James Coates

Phrenology Made Easy

James Coates

Phrenology Made Easy

ISBN/EAN: 9783337390396

Printed in Europe, USA, Canada, Australia, Japan

Cover: Foto ©Andreas Hilbeck / pixelio.de

More available books at **www.hansebooks.com**

PRICE, TEN CENTS.

Published Monthly.   By Subscription, $1.20 Per Annum.   December 1894
Entered at the New York Post Office as Second-Class Matter.   Copyright 1894 by F. M. LUPTON.

3

THE PEOPLE'S HAND BOOK SERIES

PHRENOLOGY MADE EASY.

By JAMES COATES, Ph. D., F. A. S.

F. M. LUPTON
PUBLISHER
106 AND 108 READE ST.,
NEW YORK

Phrenology Made Easy.

By JAMES COATES Ph. D., F.A.S.,

(Member of the British Phrenological Association, Etc.)

PREFACE.

HOWEVER well-started in life a man may be, he must to a certain extent be self-made. He must feel the innate aspiration of using the talents bestowed upon him.

Original capabilities are certainly bestowed by nature, yet, however great, they produce very little unless carefully cultivated. Nature bestows on all of us four-fold more talent than we develop by culture; bestows a vast amount of mentality which lies dormant for want of a true system of self-education; one founded on the science of mind. Phrenology brings us to understand the individual function of all the faculties, and by it to put them into appropriate language and action. It shows to each who would know how to strengthen his talents, how to proceed; and to those with poor opportunities how to outstrip the wealthy educated classes, who have had every advantage. It also tells those who have already acquired a profession, how to sharpen their attainments and perfect their intellectual possibilities.

The interesting volume before us embraces a series of lectures on the practical side of phrenology. Hints to the student of mental science, which are included in "Applied Phrenology," regarding various classes of heads. The Second Lecture deals with the important subject of "Measurements." From the "Size" of heads the writer very suitably passes to the "Form" of heads, and what the student is to learn therefrom. "Health" forms also a valuable chapter to the book, as also pathological researches. As we come to the Fourth Lecture we are drawn into the "Consultation Room," and are given a digest of what the latter should be; and, lastly, the writer has explained many of the queries which have come before his notice as a practical phrenologist.

We predict for the book a wide sale and no small amount of benefit to the searcher of practical science.

L. N. FOWLER.

APPLIED PHRENOLOGY.— OPENING LECTURE.

IT has been recognized that one of the most serious difficulties the student of phrenology meets in the course of his reading and investigation is the lack of information afforded by his text books or by his favorite authors on "Applied Phrenology." He is yourself with knowing man, than of setting yourself up to dictate what he should be; for he will be materialistically, spiritually, morally, or otherwise inclined, in spite of you. According to his organization and phrenological development so shall he be.

Avoid scanning the skies of your subject, assuming pedantic airs when you should walk with more humble assurance among your fellows. Study heads and faces. Never assume more than your knowledge of Human Nature through your phrenology warrants. Keep the *cui bono* of your science and the art of its application ever before you, and thus render phrenology' doubly valuable to yourself—in the reading of character, and the lessons you derive therefrom—and to others, while estimating theirs. You will thus lead and advise them to whatever practical good is to be obtained by submitting themselves to your examination. When you examine a head, if possible, never state a doubtful opinion, or should you at any time do so, give your reasons to the person examined. Most people will appreciate your candor.

The eyes of the world, *i.e.*, those who read your books, listen to your lectures, consult you for advice, your assistants, servants, wife, and children, all your world, will be upon you, ever ready to test the soundness of your views, the value of your examinations by their approximation to the truth, and their general practicability. Your mistakes (as a professional phrenologist) will be looked upon as proof positive of the insufficiency of phrenology to accomplish that which as a science it claims to be able to achieve, viz., that phrenology is not only the science of the mind—mental science, *par excellence*—but its methods are the best for discerning or reading character.

When setting yourself the task of delineating character, remember you are human, liable to err in your application of phrenological data, through your own impressionability. As on the ocean unknown currents—or currents known, for whose influence sufficient reckoning has not been made—have shipwrecked many a noble vessel, so have dominating personal influences, such as positive, magnetic natures, consciously or otherwise, affected the judgment of some phrenologists as to lead them to depart from the observance of the sure charts of this science, to make grave shipwreck of their hopes in their earlier voyages of phrenological discovery. To reduce the liability of error to a minimum, eliminate as much as possible all feelings of personal likes and dislikes (of the " Doctor Fell " order) to the person examined. Friends and critics, etc., are most likely those whom you may be called upon to examine first; with them and all others take the platform of benevolent neutrality. Remember none are so bad as they are painted, and none so good as they should be. Act as an entirely neutral party. Albeit, consulted professionally, express your opinions honestly, according to your legal phrenological attainments, without flattery, fear, or favor. The formation of such a manner,—strict faithfulness to the principles of the science: truthfulness in the expression of your opinions, description of character, nature of your advice, what not—adopted so early in your career, will be invaluable, and in the course of time will give you a name respected and honored, worthy of the science you love, and of which you now seek to be a professional exponent.

Your delineations of character may be given in this order. Tell the persons examined, 1st, What they are, what they are not; 2nd, what they should be, what they ought to have been and were not; 3rd, what they can do and do not; 4th, what they have done, and do, and should not; 5th, what they will be able to do if they make the requisite effort; 6th, what they should cultivate and restrain. In a word, what they are and what they should be.

In your examinations, never hesitate to say what phrenology says, or what you think it says. Absolute certainty can only be attained by years of experience in practical phrenology. By absolute I mean as absolute as any certainty of variable quantities can be in this world. Be careful and even painstaking in your examinations before giving expression to your opinions, no matter how intuitive, however almost sure. Never jump to conclusions, or say ought you believe your examination has not justified. When not sure, do not consider it an element of weakness to carefully re-examine the head, as necessary either to substantiate your views or to correct them; and finally, never allow the looks or hints of friends, onlookers, or of the person examined, to influence you.

You must interpret the character by the phrenology of the individual, and by no other method, however easy, gratifying, and apparently sure. Philosophically and practically, there is no safety outside of phrenology. It is the true science of mind, "every other system is defective in enumerating, classifying and telling the relations of the faculties. It undertakes to accomplish for man what philosophy performs for the external world. It claims to disclose the real state of things." It reveals man to himself. The student of mental science, as demonstrated by phrenology, cannot be ignorant of himself. This knowledge increases his responsibility, enlarges the area of his usefulness, and enhances his conception of the nobility of manhood. In and by it, he sees human nature as it is, glories in its greatness and trembles for its weaknesses. This self-knowledge is the sum of all knowledge. It is to know self, to know man, the epitome of the Universe. Phrenology has been claimed as the hand-maid of Christianity, the key to the Bible and Human Nature. I do not think that the claim is an exaggerated or excessive one.

As phrenologists (students of self or of your fellow-men) you have embarked on a noble mission and career. Your reward may not be in the applause of man, in the coin of the realm, in position, dignities, or gratified ambition. Its professorships may not be attached to our seats of learning

Nevertheless your study is a fascinating one ; its rewards are more genuine, more lasting, than those of the world. If you are enabled by your profession to make the mechanic the better man, the man the better mechanic, and all with yourself more noble and true, your mission to others and your work for yourself will not have been in vain. You will be rewarded in your very difficulties and struggles, for they shall be like the blows of the blacksmith on the tyres of the wheel, each blow perfecting its construction ; so will every difficulty fit you for your true work.

To resume : In going through life use your eyes. Phrenology is essentially a science of observation ; observation must perfect it, observation alone can detect where its methods or modes of application are faulty. While using your eyes, bring into play all the faculties represented by the organs of the anterior and coronal brain. Perception, to take cognizance of external things, such as the physiology, form, configuration, coarseness or fineness, quantity and quality of the organization. The knowing faculties, to recall the facts observed, configurations and illustration, principles of phrenology studied and their application to the facts observed, comparison and induction, to give a reason for the hope that is within you, the why and wherefore of your conclusions, based on what you have observed. Intuition, and your spiritual or moral nature, to aid you in penetrating below the surface of your observed facts, for remember, you are dealing, not with flesh and bones, but with sentient beings like yourself, whom you are endeavoring to know something about, to penetrate, to read by the outward and visible signs of their inward spiritual grace, such as temperament and quality of organization, form of body, contour of brain, as represented by the physiology, shape of head, facial form and expression. You will seek to ascertain by these signs whether they are living or merely assisting in their propensities, or in their propensities and intellectual faculties, in their moral and intellectual faculties ; or in what way their real life or soul manifests itself. You will proceed with your investigations, by observation and reflection, until no fact, no particular, escapes notice, or is considered too small to be recognized as a physical factor, determining and demonstrating character.

In shop, market, church, religious and political assembly, in friend or servant, ever be on the outlook for phrenological information. Pay special attention to the eccentric, peculiar, loud voiced, to whisperers, to the pretentious, affected, to the celebrated and notorious who may fall within the range of your vision. Keenly observe every move or manner, and as far as you can, without personal manipulation, but by observation merely, endeavor to ascertain how far such and such characteristics are made apparent in the craniology of those observed, not omitting to notice such modifying influences as health, temperament, or quality. Again, carefully notice the possible when unobserved by them; or when doting mothers are enlarging on the innumerable qualities of their beloved offspring, carefully scrutinize the formation of the heads of these little ones, and then draw your own mental conclusions. By no means neglect in your investigations the conduct and mannerisms of so-called ordinary folk, of whom the world—our world—is principally made up; and finally, take special note of the esteemed, and the vicious and criminal. Having acted upon the preceding hints, and trained your faculties of observation and powers of deduction as much as possible, then commence to train your fingers to aid your eyesight and judgment, by examining all the heads you can get to examine. Do not hurry in your examinations, and whenever you come in contact with developments similar to those, or approximating those you have observed or read about, and may have seen illustrated, see to it how far similar characteristics of craniology are borne out by similar characteristics of manner and habit, and in what degree. In this way you will cultivate what might be termed the physiognomy of phrenology, and in time, from form of face predicate form of head, and *vice versa*, and from either the character. Avail yourself of every method of arriving at character, but principally rely upon what we esteem pure phrenological methods.

"To read character correctly, it is absolutely necessary to take into consideration, not only the organs of the brain, their size, function, and combination, but the stock, health, temperament, education, and culture of the individual as well. In a word quality as well as quantity." In the foregoing you have the essence of practical phrenology. If you desire to be a successful reader of character, you must aim to convert theory into practice. No hard and fast rules can be laid down. As a practitioner, you must adopt those methods you find by practice and experience to be the best; but to aid you, I will indicate those methods which I have found to be most useful.

As an examiner, in practice, it is not only necessary to "know what you know," but to be able to "say what you know" in the most direct manner, not only in such a way as to be pleasing and satisfactory to yourself, but also to be thoroughly understood and appreciated by the person examined. It must therefore be expressed according to the ability, intelligence, receptivity, and character of your client. This is most important in the delineation of character. By it, or by the want of it, the tyro in phrenology, the glib utterer of phrenological phrases, will be detected and distinguished from the true phrenologist.

Having carefully examined the head, and taken special note of those other conditions of quality, etc., it is now necessary to express your views; but in doing so, I do not think it advisable to inform your patron that such and such an organ is large, or that it is small, according to the usual formula, viz: "benevolence is very large, therefore," etc., "amativeness is large, therefore," etc., "self-esteem is small, therefore," etc. This is the method of beginners. Whatever conclusion as to character a phrenologist comes to, from seeing " benevolence very large," " amativeness large," and " self-esteem small," the mental process by which he arrives at the sum total of character need not be expressed. The stating that such and such an organ is large, and another small, may be pleasing to the young examiner, and gratifying to the person examined, but it is of no practical value. Moreover it is misleading to the person examined, meaning anything or nothing, and, like the utterances of ancient oracles, susceptible of double interpretations. For instance it is well known that a man may have " large benevolence " and not be benevolent. It is therefore misleading to say to a person, " Sir, I find you have large benevolence," when in all probability his benevolence may be but the appendage of his vanity, the outcome of his desire, to acquire for himself a good name, praise, position; or his benevolence may be but a safety valve to his selfishness and love of ease. He gives because " he hates to be bothered," " can't stand a row," or " woman's tears." " He has no time for investigation : better give them something and let them go ; " and last though not least, " anything for peace sake," and so on. Upon such hollowness and a little cash he poses as a philanthropist—a benevolent man. In fact character cannot be predicated on the existence of a single organ unless indeed its predominance overshadow the whole. A man of large " self-esteem " may not be proud, but with " secretiveness " reserved, with " conscientiousness " and the appropriate support of the intellectual organs, dignified and just.

A phrenologist should of all persons be clear, definite, and just, neither mercilessly critical as some are, who think it is their duty to be everlastingly fault-finding, or fulsome and " buttery," as others are, " who are afraid to hurt feelings," and " who desire to make the most of a person's qualities, to encourage them," at the same time abstaining from fully stating their failings, lest they should lose their support and patronage, or that of their friends. Nor should the phrenologist be a mere numerical " bumpfeeler," one who takes a numerical and alphabetical round of the organs in order that he may oracularly inform his client of his knowledge of their location and size. All such methods should be avoided by the phrenological aspirant as unworthy of a science which more than any other speaks with certain sound as the guide of man and the interpreter of his nature.

In examining, keep the relative size, largeness, fullness, smallness, etc., of the various organs and their groups in your mind, mentally combining or balancing the same to the best of your ability. Then give the result of your reflections in simple English to your visitor. You can point out whether they are imaginative, inventive, executive, logical, argumentative, affectionate, respectful, truthful, ambitious, courageous, moral or immoral, sly, economical, musical, or mathematical, possessing a good memory or not, where most active, or most lacking. All this can be expressed in a straightforward, courteous, telling, earnest way, and will do more for phrenology, for yourself, and the person examined, than by the other method referred to. Why? You speak to the comprehension of the individual, to his or her knowledge of themselves, and to the reason—understanding—by facts, comparison, and illustrations, etc. Having gained the intellectual assent and confidence of the person by this mode of procedure, they will be all the more ready to benefit themselves by such advice as you have tendered and have deemed most suitable for them.

So much for reading character; but your reading will not be complete unless you give good advice therewith, according to the circumstances arising for its necessity. The simplest and most direct way to give advice, would be, 1st : To refer to health as affected by temperamental conditions and character, or character as affected by temperamental conditions and health. What conditions or course of habit will be most conducive to beneficial results, health, vigor, stamina, etc. Bearing in mind " that tone of mind is dependent upon vigor of organization." Whatever improves or deteriorates the latter, must be beneficial or prejudicial to the former. Then reference can be made to those organs (by name, now, if you like) whose actions are excessive, or comparatively ineffectual. Commence at the domestic instincts or faculties, and work along the base of the brain, upwards, sideways, and forward on the head, making mention of the organs upon which you wish to call special attention. Thus, you might have to say, " Self-esteem is not so full as it might be to your advantage ; endeavor to bear this in mind and place a higher estimate on yourself . . . endeavor, etc," or proceed to dwell on the importance of self-esteem as a sentiment, its value in giving dignity, resolution, quiet force, and decision to character, etc.

Again, " Approbativeness is an active and leading organ in your head. Your comparative want of " self-esteem " is unfortunate. You are ambitious, desire to be made much of, (praised, flattered, petted). You are too much influenced by censure or praise. You want quiet force and decision, etc." You may show where " approbativeness " is liable to perversion ; " the danger arising from undue sensitiveness ; love of attention," etc., when such remarks are necessary, and so on, with such combinations as may demand some words of warning and guidance. For example, moderate " self-esteem," large " approbativeness," " cautiousness," " secretiveness," large " firmness," average " conscientiousness," and large " acquisitiveness," are not at all improbable combinations. A thousand other combinations of more intricate character will arrest your attention as you grow more observant and more experienced, and will demand solution at your hands.

In this way by calling attention to the organs and their location, you can point out, what to cultivate, and what to restrain and how, in the most direct and advantageous manner. When giving your concluding advice you may with mutual benefit mention certain books, (which you may introduce) as suited for the instruction and well-being of the person examined. Sometimes there may be habits of such a character, that your delicacy, position, or that of the person examined, or the presence of other persons at the examination, may make it difficult for you to say anything in a pointed or judicious way to the patient.* The difficulty may be solved by strongly advising your client to read such and such a book. It matters little whether the work is on phrenology, tobacco, or matrimony, as long as the subject matter of the books recommended, either gives the advice you want to give, or adequately supports the advice you have already given.

Be faithful, never flatter, never speak simply to please yourself or gratify the vanity of your visitor. Never give foolish advice, " be sober-minded " and diligent in business. Do not expect of men and women other than their organization and brain development seem to indicate. At the same time do all you can to foster and encourage the good, the noble and true in all who come under your hands, by dwelling on future development in intelligence, morals, or character, business or professional success possible to each, through the cultivation or re-

straint of certain faculties, etc. Do not allow yourself to be misled by false or pretentious mannerisms but trace these characteristics at once to their seat in the brain, and account or allow for their influence at true value.

Other suggestions may be given here in passing. Always be self-possessed, collected, speak in the name of phrenology, eliminate the personal, and remember you are standing on a neutral platform. Be free and smooth of speech, adopt an illustrative, rather than an argumentative style of matter and manner in address. For one person who can appreciate a logical disquisition, ten thousand can appreciate the beauty of an illustration. Your work is to educate the masses, to lead them from what they think they know, to what you know of them, of human nature and its possibilities, at least from your standpoint. For plainness and directness of speech, sound English, you have in John Bright or C. H. Spurgeon most notable examples: what one has achieved in politics and the other in theology, you may honorably strive to do for phrenology.

As a public speaker, don't read papers (although writing makes an exact man). Study your subject well, make use of headings or notes if you will (use as few quotations as possible, and when you do let them be accurate). Deliver yourself in homely, simple, and everyday language. Speak to the people, not at them. Don't go out of your way to pulverize your opponents. State your truths and illustrate your facts, and when you can, avoid technic-

---

* It is important as the phrenologist acquires the ability to give Hygenic advice, that he should do so, and in the delineation of character to omit nothing which should be spoken about.

alities. If compelled to employ them, without apology to your audience or making use of the pedantic " that is," explain what you mean briefly and clearly.

The style of address used in the consulting room should be continued on the platform. Before commencing to lecture it is advisable to be well provided with diagrams, busts, and portraits of well-known persons, celebrated or notorious, and a good phrenological set illustrative of the temperaments and the organs. You can then lecture to the eye as well as to the ear. You will thus double your audience and secure four-fold attention. As to matter of lecture, just seek to drive home phrenological facts in their varied applications ; and last, though not least, aim to secure professional patronage. If you succeed in the first, you are most likely to succeed in the latter. A man may be a good lecturer and an indifferent examiner. In this latter department you must aim at being as perfect as possible. It is here you must make your reputation as a practical man. " A real helper to your fellows." Of course the more actual knowledge you possess of life, close contact with your fellows, habits, interests, and of trades, professions, the better you will thereby be fitted for your work.

Now as a further preliminary to practical work grind yourself well on the general principles of phrenology as set forth in the books you have read. Seek less to harmonize the differences between authorities (which are trifling of the science) than by personal investigation to satisfy your mind of the truth of these principles. Also be careful to extend your reading as opportunity may afford.

First.—Make yourself proficient in the location of the organs and their groups, on the living head (always bearing in mind that the faculties of the mind related to each other are represented by organs grouped together in the brain) so as to be able to point out unerringly the location of any organ at a moment's notice.

Second.—So as to be able to approximate to the exact size without the use of tape, accustom your eye to take measurements. If you were an artist, you would not take out "a two-foot rule," or tape line, to take the dimensions of a lady's nose before you painted her portrait. Neither should you require to do so in order to paint her mental portrait. While thus training the eye, there are some measurements which you might take to advantage, such as, 1st : The circumference measurement. Pass tape round the head over " individuality " " destructiveness," and " parental love." 2nd : The coronal height of head. Take your measurement from the lower side of the orifice of the ear (a) —*meatus auditus*—to the corresponding point on the other side of the head, over (f) " firmness." Measure from the lower side of the root of the nose (b) to the lower side of the occipital spine (c), over individuality, eventuality, firmness and parental love. These three measurements will give volume of the brain. Additional measurements can be taken such as anteriorly, from ear to ear, over individuality, to get the length or volume

1.—MORAL AND INTELLECTUAL TYPE OF HEAD.

PROFESSOR DRUMMOND.

(*Author of "Natural Law in the Spiritual World."*)

of perceptive brain, inferior anterior lobes, and from ear to ear, over causality, for the length or volume of reflective brain, superior anterior lobes. These measurements will be referred to in my next lecture.

* In taking the frontal measurement over individuality, 13 to 14 inches represents anterior lobes of great power, lesser measurements in lesser proportion, 12½ inches, a good head, 12 full, 11 average, 10 or 9, etc., cabbies, ostlers, servants, and the non-governing groups of humanity.

The average size of the head of an adult male (British) is 22 inches in circumference, with length and coronal height about 14½″, as in measurements 1, *a f a* and *b f c*. This size I would mark on register, 4 or average; 22½ inches with corresponding length and height, I should mark 5 or full; 23¼ 6 or large; 23¾ or 24, 7 or very large; 21, 3 or moderate; 20 inches, 2 or small. For an inch less in circumference, with corresponding measurement in length and height, I would give the same mark to the female head. There is in practice a difficulty here, as much will depend upon what register or chart you mark, how far full, large or small, may represent the state of

II.—WELL-BALANCED TYPE OF HEAD.

PRESIDENT PAYNE, of Nashville University.

things in reality. In this you must be guided by observation and your innate common-sense. It is advisable, whenever you can, to either give a full verbal delineation of character, or a carefully written one. In either case you will be in the best position to state what you think. Charts, registers, however carefully marked, are, to third parties who were not present at the examination, misleading.

As a phrenologist, you will take into account all the influences as represented by health, temperament, and organic quality. Physiognomy, habits, mannerism, and what not, are not absolutely necessary, but form useful auxiliaries in estimating character. Nevertheless, the size of the brain and its form, as a whole, is the rock upon which you must take your stand.

Size and form of the head as a whole, and size and form of the head in parts, may be estimated thus: Take a side view of the head, and you may divide that view into three parts or hypothetical regions thus: 1. As the region of the moral and aspiring faculties—as that part of the head above an imaginary line drawn from the upper part of (com)parison to the upper part of continuity, $\frac{1}{2}$ or $\frac{3}{4}$ of an inch from the apex of the occipital bone o a. 2. As the region of intellect—that anterior part of the head in front of a line drawn down from " cautiousness " to " alimentiveness." 3. The region of the domestic or social, and self-protective instincts in that posterior and basilier portion of the head, not included in regions 1 and 2. View these regions again from the back, front, and top of the head, so as to form a fair estimate of their size or volume. Now having an insight into a man's temperament, health, activity, excitability, quality of organization, with a careful note of the size and form of the brain as a whole, and the form, or predominance of anyone of these parts, etc., you have at once the ability to grasp the bias and the leading traits of your patron's character. Facility, in estimating details in character, will come to you as you acquire power to still further analyze these regions into their more minute sub-divisions.

APPLIED PHRENOLOGY.—SECOND LECTURE.

In my last lecture I desired to impress upon you that size (and form) of the brain is the rock upon which you must take your stand. In this I shall treat the subject more fully. All truly great men have great or large heads, but all men having great or large heads are not great men. Here you have in a nutshell a practical illustration of what we mean by quantity and quality. In the first class of heads, represented by truly great men you have not only volume, weight, or quantity of brain, but you have fineness of texture or quality as well. In the latter class, you have the quantity minus the quality. In practice you will find every type of head between these indicated. But in no instance will you find ought to mitigate or undermine the essential principle of phrenology, as indicated throughout nature, viz., " Size, other things being equal, is the measure of power." Consequently phrenologists are able to tell from the size of an organ, its power of manifestation; and from the energy of its manifestation, its relative size.

I cannot impress this too strongly upon you that size is one of the most important factors in estimating mental ability, disposition, or character. You will never find intellectual men, whose heads measure less than 21 inches in circumference, and less than 10½ inches from ear to ear, over individuality, even with fineness in quality. You may find smartness, memory for words, capacity for "cribbing" and the diluting of other men's ideas, considerable dexterity, manipulative power, and even artistic and musical tastes, but no originality, and certainly no strength of intellect, with such a brain. 22 inches is a good average size measurement for an adult male head, 22½ inches for the North American, Canadian, German, and Anglo-Celtic, and Anglo-Saxon head. You will find that the inhabitants of colder countries have heavier brains and larger heads (due allowance being made for fat and integuments, which are generally fuller and heavier in these heads than those belonging to people of more Southern latitudes).

In these regions the struggle for existence is not so great; therefore inventiveness, constructiveness, executiveness, and the offensive, defensive, and sustaining faculties of the mind are not so much called forth in that struggle. The Scotchman, who contends with mists, a humid atmosphere, a low temperature, and an unkindly soil for sustenance, will have a sturdier physique and larger brain than his Erse and neighbor and kinsman in Ireland. The French peasant and Italian lazaroni will have smaller heads than their compeers in Great Britain and Ireland, or their descendants in North America, or the Inhabitants of Northern Europe, the Germans, Fins and Russians. It is also worthy of note, persons descended from and those who have habituated themselves to out-door pursuits, have on average larger brains than those who have been accustomed to sedentary and mental pursuits.

As already stated, 22 inches is a good average size, with 11½ inches from ear to ear over individuality for an adult man. Vigor and stamina of brain increase, with weight and size, up to 24 and 24¼ inches in circumference measurements. If there is great fineness of organization, or even excessive mental development, at this size or over, there is a suspicion of disease, which you should be on your alert to detect. The brain of an idiot may be perfectly healthy, but will be found either defective in form, poor, or coarse in quality, whether large or small in quantity. In the major number of cases it will be found defective in form, coarse in grain, and deficient in quantity. In the majority of cases idiocy absolutely arises from want of brains. With 18 inches circumference measurement and under, with the brain correspondingly small, and massed principally in the base and occiput, no matter how fine the organization, good the quality, or healthy the brain, you may again become suspicious of incapacity and want of power, if not for positive imbecility, you will certainly be justified in looking for it.

These measurements, with an inch to half-an-inch less, will apply equally to the female brain. It is not true that the female brain attains its maximum size and weight at 11 years, and the male brain at 14 years of age, as stated by some physiologists. The brain develops rapidly in childhood, and increases gradually to manhood. During adult age, visible increase of brain has been detected up till 40 years of age. The head of a boy at birth in this country averages about 12 inches, at six months it is 15 inches, at twelve months 17 inches, and then makes slow progress up till 27 years of age. During this time the form of the brain alters, as well as becomes enlarged in volume. There is an increased development of the perceptives, knowing, reflective, moral, and semi-refining faculties, as suggested in the accompanying outline, fig. iii. Here you see at a glance the importance of size—size marking that difference in volume and form, and in contour which distinguishes at once the perfected male head from the immature one of childhood. The size of the brain, other things being equal, is the measure of its power—that is, claiming nothing more for phrenology than to say, the larger a piece of iron or wood, the greater its relative strength compared with smaller pieces of iron and wood of the same quality.

If a bar of iron was ten times as

III.—INFANT TO ADULT TYPES OF HEADS.

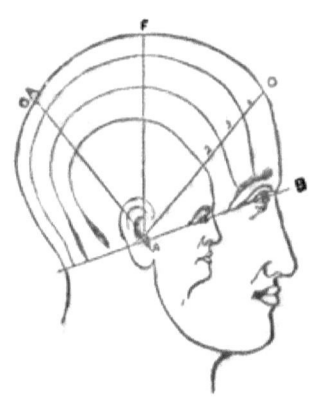

Exhibiting change of size and form with corresponding **brain** developments.

strong as a log of wood ten times the size of the iron, such a fact would not alter this proposition ; or that a log of oak, only half the size of a log of pine, should prove to have twice the durability and strength than that possessed by the pine, should not surprise you any more than some men, like Gambetta, with 40.9-oz. brain, should lord it over French boors, with coarse 50-oz. brains, or dandies for that matter, with small and uncultured fine brains. It is true the oak and pine are both wood ; but it is the texture or quality of the wood peculiar to each which makes the essential difference. A little man may be stronger than a big man ; or, what is more likely, a little woman may be more lively and spirited than a big woman : that does not affect our fundamental principle. The conditions are not equal. In this phrenology does nothing more than to place man and his brain under the universal

law of size. The objections brought
by opponents to phrenology under this
head, or about their own heads, are
peurile in the extreme ; too frequently
the objectors draw upon their imagination for their facts, or assume for
phrenology what has never been
claimed for it by phrenologists. Some
objectors would have us believe with
Esquirol, and maintain that no size or
form of head or brain is indicative of
idiocy or talent ; but, as a matter of
observation, small heads (if any) indicate the greatest talent and force of
character. Illiterate bricklayers and
ignorant butchers, driviling idiots and
demented shoemakers, are trotted out,
whose brain-pans had enough capacity
for two ordinary philosophers, whose
brains tipped the scale from 65 to 70
ozs. ; while your Gambettas and Galls
barely turned the scale at 42 ozs.
And at least one brilliant general,
Lord Chelmsford (whose mediocre
supply of brains has not been weighed
yet) has only $20\frac{1}{2}$ inches circumference
measurement of head. In fact, for
such is the force of this argument, it
would be an advantage (to the War
Office, I suppose) if our Sir Garnet
Wolseley had less brains. You may
here it stated that certain animals or
men with large brains have less intelligence than other certain animals or
men with smaller brains. The whole
of these statements are too often
founded upon mere conjecture, and
when not so they present carelessness
of observation and thoughtlessness of
expression on part of the authors.
Let us examine the position for a moment : Do phrenologists predicate

character upon large heads and foreheads merely ? or upon simply size
or weight of brain, regardless of other
considerations ? Is Lord Chelmsford
to be compared with our " only General ? " What kind of intelligence in
the animals or men do they refer to ?
How often are mere instincts and propensities confounded with the opera-
tion of intellect, reason, identity,
memory, and what not ?

Upon investigation these expressions, instead of telling against phrenology, are actually in its favor. For
instance, does the forehead present, in
addition to a broad and high front,
depth of frontal mass, *i. e.* length of
head in front of the ears? Is it really
a large forehead of breadth, height and
depth, and if so, what is the quality of
organization, coarse or fine, obtuse or
acute ? How often is it, the individual is actually " shallow-pated," having breadth and height but no depth
of forehead, being, *i. e.* actually fore
shortened in length of anterior brain-
fibre, as in *a, b, c,* figure iii. The phrenologist can soon settle these points,
much more readily than a prejudiced
flippant objector. Take another instance—the forehead may overhang,
giving " thumbed in " perceptives,
showing plenty of brain in reality, but
" bad form," an unbalanced head in
fact. The excess of the reflectives over
the perceptives giving much learning,
theory, and disposition to philosophize,
but little practicality. Or there may
be an excess in the perceptives over
the reflectives, which may give plenty
of idle observation, vulgar staring
without adequate reason, quickness of

action, plenty to say, but little wisdom, little thoughtfulness or consideration for others. All these variations of form must be considered. You are to notice that mere size of brain indicates brain-power only (as a twelve-horse boiler will generate more steam than one half its capacity) size of brain in ever particular you detect, upon actual examination size will bear you out. You must look for something more than an apparently large forehead for intelligence, ability, etc. You must look for a beautiful head (a harmonized and balanced head, phrenologically proportioned and well made, not

IV., V.—CIRCUMFERENCE MEASUREMENT OF HEADS—INTELLECTUAL AND CRIMINAL TYPES.

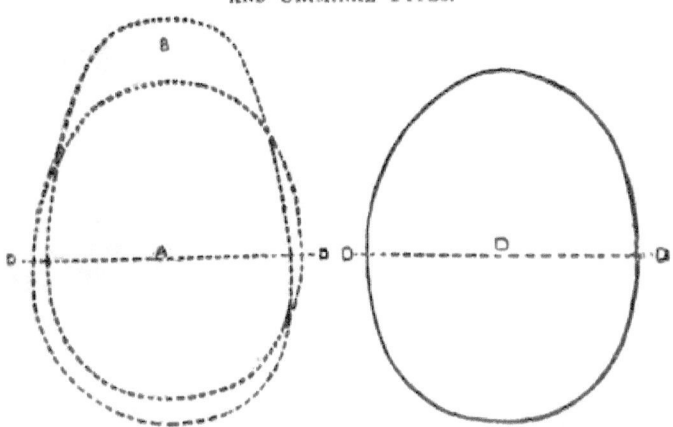

Fig. iv.—*a*. GUITEAU, the murderer. *b*. GARFIELD, the victim. *dd*. A hypothetical line drawn from ear to ear to distinguish the anterior from the posterior brain mass. Fig. v.—*d*. DEANE, the murderer. *dd*. The hypothetical line, showing the enormous posterior brain mass.

part, in what particular direction. A man like an animal may have a large mass of brain, and yet not manifest much intelligence; but both will exhibit power of some sort or other. If the "animal organs" predominate (as exhibited in the width of the brain in the basilar region of the skull) so will there be a corresponding exhibition of the animal instincts and propensities manifested in the character of the possessor of these organs. This is the invariable connection between the size and manifestation. In what-

lacking in width, height, length or form, no outrageous or inartistic outlines) to discern the really able man and good woman. True greatness, intellectual, moral, social and sympathetic manhood is not to be found in men with heads irregular in formation, with foreheads "villainously low," or having foreheads which protrude and overhang; but in men whose organization indicates good quality, and whose heads are of good size, well-formed, and harmoniously balanced—I will now resume

OUR TALK ABOUT MEASURE-MENTS.

To the theoretical, but conscientious student of phrenology, these brain measurements are a constant source of bewilderment and distress. He wants to weigh, balance and "tot up" the

VI.—BACK VIEW OF HEADS—MORAL AND CRIMINAL TYPES.

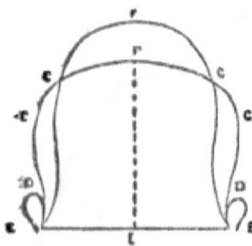

Narrow and high head—GOSSE, the benevolent. Broad and low head —PATCH, the murderer.

human faculties with mathematical precision, or if endowed with less ability, as a grocer would so many pounds of soap at so much a pound, total amount so-and-so. You are not dealing in such dead and plastic material, neither are you dealing with primary elements in chemistry, nor mathematical propositions, but with living souls, human beings whom you are trying to understand by the " outward and visible signs " they present of their " inward and spiritual grace," as marked on the outward walls of their physical being, for which purpose the brain, in its volume, and contour, and quality, is the surest index.

It is well to make all your measurements with a steel or strong linen tape line, which will not deceive you by stretching. Continue your measurements until the eye and hand are sufficiently educated to be able to make sufficient approximations for practical purposes without its use.

Take your first measurement over the base of the brain, around the head, at *c, d, c,* for circumference measurement, denoting "power and force." From *e, oa, e,* for second circumference measurement, denoting " intelligence and force." These measurements ought to be about equal. In practice you will find the first measurement the largest, as a rule. In pushing active business men you will find the lower measurement exceed the upper by half to three quarters of an inch. Thus, in the above head, $22\frac{1}{2}$ inches, *c, d, c,* (perceptives and executiveness); 22 inches, *e, oa, e,* (reflectives and re-

VII.—LITERARY TYPE OF HEAD.

W. T. STEAD, Editor *Pall Mall Gazette.*

straint); would be a favorable measurement for a wide-awake commercial man, and so on in proportion. Twenty-one and a half and $22\frac{1}{2}$ in a literary or scholastic man would be favorable for his work. Twenty-three and $23\frac{1}{4}$ for a man of science would not be too much over weight. But 23 at *e, oe, e*, and 22 at *c, d, c*, would be unfortunate, larger disproportions more so, indicating more of the theoretical than the practical, etc.

The measurements from *a* to *a*, over *f*, should be about the same as from *b*, at the root of the nose to *o, c* (taken over *f*), where the perceptives *a, c, a*, and the reflective *a, e, a*, developments are more marked than on the above head. The frontal and posterior measurement *b* to *o, c*, over *f*, may exceed that of *a, f, a*, by half-an-inch to an inch. This would indicate that the social, moral, aspiring, and intellectual developments are greater than those of the purely executive and selfish faculties. Where the head is proportionately high, as in this head, the person will be highly moral in tone and feeling; but when it is much higher than it is broad, as in this head, the person may be amiable, but will also be possessed with a strong sense of justice, which may be exhibited in a fault-finding and censorious manner. Its excess in this case leads to exacting extremes and censoriousness in the government and direction of others, as well as a prominent feeling that there are few persons who can do anything as well as himself He will be troubled by trifling circumstances. The positive and excitable elements in charac-

ter will lead to extremes and inconsistencies. More width than height often indicates a lack of moral feeling, there being greater secretiveness, acquisitiveness, destructiveness, and cautiousness than moral and spiritual development. Such a head, associated with a low type of organization, is certainly a criminal one, detected or otherwise. The height of the head should be about the same as its width—for instance, if

VIII.—Diplomatic and Financial Type of Head.

M. Romero, Mexican Minister to the United States of America.

the height from *c* to *f*, is 6 inches, the width from *c* to *c* should be 6 inches. If the measurements from *c* to *c*, or "cautiousness" to "cautiousness" is less than that from *d* to *d*, or "destructiveness" to "destructiveness," it will indicate that the restraining elements are not as powerful as the executive. In the above head the reverse is the case. In figure vii. the moral and intellectual predominates. The following measurements may be found useful to take in addition to those already given: Anterior measurements from *a* to *a*, over *e*, for the perceptives, say 12½; *a* to *a*, over *e*, for reflectives, say 13½ inches; *a* to *a*, over *g*, for intuitive or semi-intellectual measurement, say 14½ inches; *a* to *a*, over *f*, say 15 inches; and 11½ inches from *a* to *a*, over the apex of the occipital bone; 15½ inches from *b* to *oc*, over *f*, with 1st circumference measurement of *c*, *d*, *c*, of 22½ inches, and 2nd circumference measurement, *e*, *oa*, *e*, 22 inches, you would get a fine specimen of a good head, such as you might meet in daily practice as an editor, reporter, teacher, accountant, and professional pursuits requiring activity, versatility, and application.

To measure a head, you may possibly adopt your own method, that of Combe's, or those in general practice, whichever you find best; or you can adopt the following in practice, thus :—

1st measurement, *c*, *d*, *c*.

2nd   "   *e*, *oa*, *e*.

3rd   "   *a*, to *a*, over *c*, or individuality.

4th measurement, *a*, to *a*, over *e*, or causality.

5th measurement, *a*, to *a*, over *g*, or intuition.

6th measurement, *a*, to *a*, over *f*, or firmness.

7th measurement, *b*, to *oc*, over *f*, or firmness.

Take a good look at the head, first the back view—as in outline—and take in at a glance the width of brain as indicated by the size of the head, and see whether it is wider at *d*—destructiveness—or at *c*—cautiousness. And then the front view—see whether it is widest at constructiveness or at cautiousness—or vice versa. Next *take in* the side view, and impress upon the mind the relative size of your primary sub-divisions and the size of the head as a whole. There are the sub-divisions, as suggested by Combe, which doubtless approximate more to the truth in nature than those I have already marked out for practical purposes. You will see whether your patient has the most brain—back, above, or in front of his ears. *His character must correspond* with the formation. Measure your head carefully, take in the *size** thoroughly, do all this quietly and carefully before you venture on the expression of opinion. If satisfied with your observation and measurements you are on safe ground—there can be no more " ifs " and " buts "; proceed with your description (minding previous hints) and you cannot go far wrong.

Ability to measure the head with correctness or to estimate the health or otherwise of the brain, will come in time with careful observation and practice. In examining heads travel cautiously from what you know absolutely to be true—for the rest *feel your way* carefully, as phrenology un-

* In the Practical Application of Phrenology, it is the size of each organ in proportion to the others *in the* head of the *Individual Manipulated*, and not the *absolute size*, or the size in reference to any standard head, that determines the predominance of particular talents or dispositions.— E. T. Craig

folds the character to you. Some phrenologists have a definite method of examining a head. Messrs. Donovan, Combe, and Wells have given their methods, while the Fowlers, Weaver, and Story have thrown out

IX.—ARISTOCRATIC AND DIPLOMATIC TYPE OF HEAD.

SIR LIONEL S. SACKVILLE WEST, Late British Representative at Washington, U. S. A.

valuable suggestions. It has been left largely for each practitioner to adopt his own style. I always make it a point to strike at the defects in character to commence with. Now as these vary very much, it will be seen my method of reading character will depend upon the character to read. I think this is the most reasonable plan, and suggest it to your consideration. I will refer to this again.

In my first lecture, I roughly divided the brain into three hypothetical regions (unknown therefore in cerebral physiology), nevertheless an invaluable aid in examining heads—1st, the region of the moral and aspiring faculties; 2nd, the region of the intellectual faculties; 3rd, the region of the domestic faculties. I propose to further subdivide these into eight smaller regions or groups:—1st, or moral region, &c.,—*a*, intuitive, or semi-intellectual, forming the boundary line between spiritual perceptions, intuition, and pure reason; *b*, the religious and spiritual; *c*, egoistic or aspiring organs. 2nd, or intellectual region, into *e*, perceptives (and external senses); *f*, literary, and *g*, reasoning groups. 3rd, or domestic region, into *h*, domestic, and *i*, selfish propensities. The natural divisions of the skull afford some assistance. The domestic propensities are covered by the occipital bone; the selfish sentiments almost by the temporal bone; the perceptives, reflectives, and knowing faculties by the frontal bone. At its superior it also covers the semi-intellectual faculties. The moral and spiritual faculties are covered by the parietal bones, superiorly and posteriorly, while inferiorly they cover such organs of the propensities as are not covered by the temporal bones. This rough outline must be corrected by you in detail. In examining the head you will not only see what region predominates, but also what subdivision, and then what organ of the subdivision—activity by size; size indicating the activity.

In some instances you may find heads pretty equally balanced, giving you the same measurement from the orifice of the ear—over "amativeness" as over the perceptives, over continuity as over the reflectives, over firmness as over to *oc.* I do not think such uniformity in our present civilization favorable to marked worth or character. In low and diseased organizations, in proportion as the circumference measurement approximates to the circle the criminal type of head is pronounced. There is much in this form of head which requires study. Guiteau, Deane, and Patch, the murderer, see Fig. iv., v., and vi., approximate to this type. Compare them with the outline presented by Gosse *e*, and Garfield, *b*, the philanthropists. These heads are not mere coincidents, but rather awkward facts, for good men to deal with who see no relationship between organization and cranial formation to crime and virtue; awkward stars, if fallen ones, for theological telescopes to discover, or modern Paduan philosophers to argue out of existence.

National heads have their national characteristics in size, which correspond to the national traits by which they are distinguished. The German head is 1½ inches longer than its width : as a people they are given to ease, sitting and thinking, sturdy and phlegmatic. The French head is about 1½ inches longer than it is wide. The German head presents the vital-mental and motive-mental temperament ; they are slow to arouse, but when aroused they are like a ponderous machine set in motion ; they are capable of doing great execution, and

have furnished the foremost thinkers —philosophers, divines, physicians, and soldiers—veritable leaders in the world. The French are more energetic, excitable, and volatile, with the mental and mental-vital temperaments : they have greater vivacity, but less stamina than their more stolid neighbors. The English head is about 1½ inches longer than wide—that is to say, if 6½ inches wide between the ears it would be 8 inches long from the frontal semus to the apex of the occipital bone. The typical British head exhibits the best blends : Norse, Scandinavian, German, and Celtic. In quality, form and size, indicating firmness, executiveness, tenacity of purpose—intellectual and enthusiastic. The American head approximates to the English and French head. It has less veneration and continuity than the English and more than the French ; exhibiting more versatility than the English, but not so volatile or as excitable as the French. The Beecher head, or those of Lincoln and Garfield, would less represent the American head than John Bright would the English. The Scotch head, 1¾ to 1¾ longer than the width, presenting not less executiveness or firmness than the English head, but more forethought, shrewdness, slowness, and caution ; the prevailing temperaments being mental-motive and motive-mental.

While I do not think I have said anything new or exhaustive on this subject, I have driven at the *principle* of size to show you its importance in estimating character, and I have not by any means ignored the importance of quality in doing so. I shall be satisfied if you can feel you have a rock under your feet, a 'vantage ground, from which you may with safety calmly look around you and take your observations all the more securely.

Men and women are at best but children of older growth, the animal and spiritual are fearfully and wonderfully mixed in each human being, "Scratch the Russian and you will find the Tarter;" delve into human nature deep enough, and you will find the same weakness underlying all. "There are none perfect, no not one," nor none so low, but a spark of their evil life will shine through some clink of their "earthly tabernacle," if you only know where to look for it and bring it into conscious life. True, there are many defective and depraved human organizations in this world— sans soul, heart or head—lacking spirituality, affection, and intelligence for all that is good, or having one thing and lacking another. To comprehend them fully, or uplift them, may be "beyond the art of man;" don't despair, but believe that deep down in each, although hidden from your sight under the débris of all that is sensual, devilish, and earthly, there is a priceless gem in each human casket (however untoward and unkempt that casket may be) that shall yet shine in the sunlight of Eternal Goodness "sometime, somewhere," when the fetters of all things vile— hereditarily cursed and depraved mortal coil—shall be removed for ever. If this is not so, then assuredly if *imitation* proves the "descent

of man," our node progenitors were hairy animals, who walked on all fours, lived in aborial retreats, wagged their ears at pleasure, and wringled their scalps at will, and whose habits were monkeyish and unseemly, whose be all and end all—was mud. If this is science then our faith runs—where this science neither follows nor directs —and declares to our inward vision the dignity of manhood and the nobility of his heritage, in spite of that materialism which makes man the heir of protoplasm and the co-heir of apes, and in the end converts him into first-class manure, as the final and highest use of his evolution. Believe me (although I cannot enter here upon the theme) phrenology leads not from God or soul, but leads to them, or else "Know Thyself" is but a "tinkling cymbal and sounding brass."

Few men are great, fewer still true men. There are few great and true, living geniuses, burning and shining lights. It is perhaps well for the world that it is so. Like seers of old the truly inspired live in the open air, wear raiments of camel's hair, eat locusts and wild honey, and are sacrificed to the whims of dancing strumpets, and by those whom they would teach or reprove. The world prefers glamour, glitter, passing shadows, and "the pomp and circumstance of war," to beauty of soul, and the godliness of sobriety, and the patience of love. Hence philosophers burn brimstone and talk of "sweetness and light," and when ignored by the busy bees of the world's hive, become the intellectual dandies, who amuse, while they are petted by an idle, pedantic and fashionable society which feeds itself upon "words, words, words." Poets loose their heads in coronets, in fulsome flattery or the flowing bowl. Finding "life not worth living," they end it by arsenic, like Chatterton; by hysteria and sensuality, like Byron; when they do not end their reputation by impurities and agnosticism like Swinburne.

Self-esteem and approbativeness have often stimulated to madness the the unbalanced geniuses of bye-gone days. The world feels their loss, having been affected by their meteor-like brilliancy, ten or twenty decades afterward holds their centenary and applauds itself or its goodness, while treating itself to fêtes and galas. It is all the while repeating the treatment of cruelty or adulation to their adulated heroes, worthy or unworthy successors.

Where few are great — geniuses, originators, creators and inventors— many are talented, more balanced in their organization, they are content to execute faithfully their allotted task in life, according to the position, opportunity, special talents or gifts.

The great mass of mankind are mimics, ready to respond to the most predominating influence for good or ill, which marks the boundary of their life. Others are like sheep who flee or jump barriers, because and only because some other sheep more daring or more foolish has led the way; the surrounding social influences of some men making or marring their lives forever—creatures under the guiding influences of one or two organs, living in

one or two spots of their nature and vegetating on the rest, "cribbed, coffined and confined" by the rude instincts of childhood and barbarism, or worse still, modern civilization.

The full-souled, full-orbed man, "the perfect man" is the dream of the Christian. The man who lives truly in every department of his being by use and not abuse is the "coming man" —phrenologist—who, if a genius or talented, will not be less, but more the man.

There are two other classes— "Hewers of wood and carries of water" and fools, the latter including the idle, insand, and idiotic. The industrial and mechanical classes may be included in the former : they, with the "talented," "are the salt of the earth," the preservers of the economic, political, and religious world. The rest when not mere ornaments, "leather and prunella," are "shadows by the way." These make life beautiful or miserable by their fitful contrasts.

In all classes you will find vices and virtues, strong passions, loves and desires, stimulating, and organs to stimulate; those for whom fame has no seduction, duty has; those who will not labor for glory, and dare destruction at a cannon's mouth for a lady's smile and knighthood, will, perhaps, be only too glad to work for something to eat. Those for whom the cooing of the babe, or a mother's winning voice, a wife's tender love, have no meaning, may pile up for themselves "gold, silver, and precious stones." Some are stimulated to action by love, fear, envy, ambition, or necessity;

some, by the love of life and the necessity to preserve it; others, by the love of others. All are influenced by some consideration—whether that be love of self, life, or wife, of children, friends, or the helpless and outcast; or perchance by some Utopian dream or grovelling instinct; in a word, by appetites, passions, affections, by pride, glory, and the desire to excel, by reason, by moral and spiritual inspiration —all are consciously or unconsciously influenced or directed. As it is written, " None can live or die unto themselves."

It will be your duty and privilege to analyze all these, and help this wonderful being—man—as far as lies within the province of your influence, to know himself and his surroundings; to suit his surroundings and his constitution—mental and physical; his circumstances to his enlightened will; to live his honest life by living his fullest life, in subordinating the animal to the spiritual and intellectual—and walk erect, a man.

PRACTICAL INSTRUCTION.

• For general reading peruse " Kirk's Anatomy," " Trall's Physiology," Dr. Nichol's " Human Physiology," and Sir Charles Bell's " Anatomy of Expression."

Lessons on Theory. Read up Combe, Wells, Fowler, on the classification of the faculties. Also learn the definitions of the faculties, as given by A. T. Story in his " Manual of Phrenology," as you would axioms in Euclid, or grammatical rules.

Lessons in Observation. Make yourself acquainted with the three major regions of the brain—" animal propensities," " moral sentiments," and " intellectual faculties "—and the sub-sections of these regions in groups and organs; and learn to localize them thoroughly on a blank bust or the living head. Accustom your eyes to make approximate measurements of the heads of persons you meet in friendship and business.

Lessons on Practice. Form an estimate of a person's manner of address—lecturer or minister—by seeing them on platform or pulpit, by their heads. Note whether they are influenced by large or small cautiousness, large or small benevolence, large or small destructiveness; whether musical, witty, anecdotal, dramatic, severe, or sympathetic, &c.

APPLIED PHRENOLOGY.—
THIRD LECTURE.

x.—Six Heads Drawn to One Scale. Taken from Casts from Nature.

1.—Dr. CHALMERS, Eminent Divine.
2.—Sir ISAMBERT MARC BRUNEL, F. R. S., Engineer of the Thames Tunnel.
3.—EUSTACHE, The Benevolent Negro.
4.—GOTFRIED, Murderess of 14 Persons.
5.—STEVENTON, Pugilist and Murderer.
6.—AMSTERDAM IDIOT, 25 years of age.

HAVING considered size, at some

length, form necessarily comes next under review. When you notice the size of a man's head, the next thing to arrest your attention is its form. Combe has remarked: " The form of the head is not less important to phrenologists than size."

Although I propose to glance at the influence of temperament on character further on, I refer to it here for the purpose of pointing out that the form or shape of the head invariably corresponds to the temperament, and it will, therefore, always indicate the predominant physiology of the individual. The dominant physiology or temperament will invariably give its bias to character. The form of the head will also indicate the particular direction of that bias. To delineate character from a plaster cast or skull should not present any great difficulty, as some suppose, on account of not discerning the temperament of the original. Such a statement can only be the result of lack of observation. Form is ever an invaluable key to temperament. Form has also an invariable relation to quality—i. e., the fineness, delicacy, tension, denseness or coarseness of organism, structure or physiology. Whoever saw a fine organization, with prognathous jaws, receding and low forehead, and pendulous abdomen? or a fine organization, with disproportionately long arms, and large hands, and large and flat feet to general build, and so on? More correct observation on the part of objectors would soon rectify prevalent errors on this point. The size and form of the head, presented, even by a plaster cast,

would be invaluable indicators to a phrenologist, not only of temperament, but of quality of organization. For instance, in Fig. X., 4, 5, and 6, indicate lower types of organization and temperament than 3, 2, and 1, which ascend in quality of structure, as they increase in cranial development, or perfection of form. Form of head corresponds to temperament. If the nervous physiology or mental temperament predominates, it gives width and fulness to the superior anterior lobes of the brain, and therefore fulness and breadth to the forehead, a periform contour to the face, corresponding expansiveness superiorly to the semi-refining organs. When the arterial or sanguine physiology, or healthy vital temperament predominates, the base of the brain is more fully rounded and larger than in the mental or foregoing, while not so full in the superior brain, the perceptive, social, and executive faculties will be marked in character,—this form of the vital giving a healthy stimulus to the mental faculties. When the nervous physiology, or the lymphatic form of the vital temperament predominates, the circulation is sluggish; the superior anterior development of the brain as seen in the form of the head is not so full, while the parietal and posterior organs are more marked than in the former temperament; the face is rounded, and there is a round configuration of the head : the sensuous and social faculties—which indicate love of life, foods and drinks, ease, and quiet enjoyment—are marked. The osseous and muscular physiology, or motive temperament, gives height rather than width to the head; there is less of the activity of the mental, and warmth and enthusiasm of the vital, but greater steadiness in action, conjoined with greater durability and tenacity in disposition: these characteristics agree with the influence of the aspiring organs—the egotistical group—which are marked in this temperament. There are various phases of this temperament, as it is modified by others; the form or physiognomy alters, of course, with the modification. There are the osseous, and the muscular, and the nervous forms, and so forth, of the motive temperament —the harsher outlines of the first being modified as it becomes less and the others become more marked.

In point of fact, there are as many temperaments as there are organs in the body. It would be difficult, therefore, even with the aid of diagrams, to point out the ever-varying forms which the intricate combinations of the various temperaments give, and by which forms they are detected. You will find for practical purposes the simple classifications given in our text-books are best. Mr. Burns gives an interesting reading of the temperaments in his English edition of Weaver's Lectures on Phrenology, and both Mr. Story and Mr. Wells depart from the old English classification and the new American one. There is much to be said in favor of all these views. It is best that each one should read for himself. If temperament is indicated by form, head, as well as of body, you can readily see from that form

whether a brain is active or otherwise; a large brain will be less active than a smaller one; if its temperament be inferior, it must have necessarily less activity, with the lymphatic form of the vital temperament, than it would have with the sanguine form of the same temperament, less activity with the osseous than muscular form of the motive temperament. In judging the relative power of the various groups or organs in the same head, temperament or physiology need not be considered, as all the organs of the head must be similar in temperament; therefore, what you may know of their power, action, or function, will be indicated to you by the size and form presented by them. I may venture on a word of caution here. While dwelling on form—(we have so-called model heads or busts, which serve the same useful purpose in phrenology as maps in the study of geography, or diagrams in physiology)—there is no such thing as a special form of head or model head. In nature there are no two heads alike, either in size, form, or quality (to say nothing of the environment, or opportunity, education, religious training, and what not, possible to each). Therefore, it is necessary not to predicate character, talent, or capacity, to any special form of head or model, and to depreciate the possession of character, talent, or capacity in the direct ratio of the departure of the head (examined) from the same model head, or standard of phrenological excellence. The model head is but a fanciful creation of what the coming or perfect man is expected to possess, but in point of fact, its existence must be hypothetical, and for hypothetical uses "point a moral and adorn a tale." The practical phrenologist can only deal with heads as he finds them.

A modern divine has declared " Jesus Christ was man at His climax." Mr. Fowler has said, "Man at his climax is man perfected physically and mentally." That Jesus* was "the Perfect Man " in structure, organization, and cerebral development, will be admitted. And as being so He would have the most perfect head. So far as man has departed or degenerated from that model head and type of perfection, it is assumed his inferiority in character, physically, mentally, morally, spiritually, and socially, would be proportionate. This style of argument, while it furnishes problematical ground for debate, it does not at the same time furnish or serve any useful purpose. The head of Jesus was essentially His own. It may not be possible for men to have heads like His. God, in His infinite wisdom, through His creative, executive, and sustaining laws, has ordered it otherwise. His (Jesus's) head and organization were most perfect for the manifestation of Christ's love, life-work, and character in the world. As there can only be one Christ, so there can

only be His particular form of organization (and head) for the manifestation of Himself. As it is with Him, so it is with us : according to our organization (and head), so will be our life and character. The Saviour of mankind was limited by His humanity and by His environment, and so are we. He learned to go about His Father's business—and so may we, whether we have one talent or ten, according to " our several ability." The form of our head will indicate it or them; and our ability for manifesting the same shall be as perfect in its exhibition of our character, work, and place in the race—national, local, or personal—as His was for His appointed work.

Every character must be judged by its own head, or the brain by which or through which that character is manifested, and not by comparison to or with some other head, real or imaginary, which shall be set up as a model head. What each man or woman can do, or is capable of doing, will be within the limits of their own organization, brain development, form, and not beyond it. Form is the universal language of physiology, constitution, and being ; by it, and through it, we see and interpret nature—man or monkey, beast or bird, in connection therewith. Form has its relation to intellect and character. With variation of form we associate variety of talent, capacity, and disposition. If one man manifests more energy and efficiency in a given direction than another, it must not be assumed he is superior, mentally or morally, to that other, since it may be found that in certain directions the

---

* Publius Lentulus, in his letter to the Roman Senate, describes Jesus "as being of full stature rather tall, with hair the color of a chestnut when fully ripe, smooth to the ears, and then curling, and flowing down upon the shoulders; in the midst of the forehead a stream, or partition of hair. His beard was of the same color, and very full, but not long. His eyes grey and clear His nose and mouth of a form such as no description on earth could represent them. His forehead was without wrinkle or spot; His posture, one of gracefulness and symmetry beyond description."

second may manifest talents and capabilities, and in them throw the first completely in the shade. But wherein each severally excels, the cranial formation shall correspond therewith. Thus a sluggish, inactive life, cannot be found with large "vitativeness," "hope," and moderate "cautiousness." Nor an active life with moderate "vitativeness," "destructiveness," "hope," and large "cautiousness." The energy and executiveness of one man may be the natural expression of "firmness," "self-esteem," "hope," and "destructiveness"; of another that of "hope," "approbativeness," "destructiveness," and "combativeness." The former will be fired to action by an entirely different motive from that of the latter, and the goal of their ambition, as far apart as the poles. What the motives may be, or incentives to action, will be as readily discernible in the form of the head. While we are careful to exclude the hypothetical model, or standard model head of well-meaning but imaginative souls, it is no less certain that good heads have such characteristics in form which distinguish them from such as are bad or indifferent. This, however, requires neither argument nor illustration to demonstrate. The mere suggestion should be sufficient for all practical purposes. Thus, for the exercise of sound judgment, penetration, cognizance of the useful or useless, expedient or inexpedient, there must be more than a fair intellectual development of brain. That for energy and force, there must first be that basis in the constitution best adapted to give them. In every instance the intellectual capacity, and the energy and force, will be indicated by the form and appearance of the individual; the size and contour of the brain, as indicated by the skull, the surest index. Whether we note our politicians, statesmen, ministers, or business men, who are to the forefront in their special spheres in life, the men who have risen and struck out, so to speak, above and beyond the ordinary file of society, and become its rank or leaders, we find the greatest variety of cranial formation, of constitution, temperament, or physiology and form. For instance, in politics how dissimilar Disraeli, Gladstone, Bright, and Parnell. In religion, Spurgeon, Parker, Caird, and Story. The greatest points of difference or excellence of talent and capacity, corresponding with those differences of quality, constitution, and cranial formation, detectable to the eye of the skilled observer and phrenologist. Each head must be judged on its own merits, by its own form, and by the constitution of the individual, and not by attempting to adjust them to some given standard of brain form, and physical quality of organization.

HEALTH.

In giving a delineation of character, we do not overlook certain important conditions which indicate quality—as size indicates quantity, or form the temperament. One of the most important of these conditions is Health.

In estimating how healthy a person is, and how far their present condition of health may or does affect the powers of their mind or the manifestation of their character—intellectually, morally, and what not—the phrenologist does not require to have the training of the physician or medical expert; nor is it necessary for him to adopt or imitate their methods of diagnosis or solemn freemasonry of technical nomenclature in expression. If you cannot tell at a glance whether your patron is healthy or not, neither can you tell what the predominating physiology or temperament is; nor can you tell what is the quality of the organization, what the form or size of the brain may be, or what the most prominent characteristics of the individual are. If you cannot tell these you must either give up your notion to become readers of character until you have well trained your powers of observation and reflection, or remain ignorant and pretentious phrenologists. Better be an honest bricklayer.

Health of mind and body is essential to success in life. You can read better with sound eyes than sore ones. Think better without a headache than with one. Enjoy the services of the temple without a colic than with one. " Fulness of bread " may puff up, but hunger seldom renders one gracious or grateful (although by it the Prodigal came to himself, and the fear of it has been a powerful incentive to industry and invention). Dyspeptic sermons, and the penitential utterance of the drunkard's morning, cannot be considered wholesome, sound, or healthy transactions.

A bilious man in the midst of a bilious world can see no good in anybody, and very little in himself. " Livered," " hipt," and jaundiced people are never optimists. You might as well dilate on the beauties of sunset tints on the western skies, or the magnificent variegations of color caused there by the restless, gorgeous, and ever-rolling ocean to a sea-sick passenger, as to expect expressions of gratitude, admiration, and delight from such people. In theory, they ought to be " rejoicing in affliction," " glorying in tribulation ; " but, in fact, they don't ; " it's agin natur." Offended nature punishes, and all suffering is grievous. A powerful mind cannot be manifested by or through a weak brain, or brilliancy of talent—special talent —through defective organs. It is impossible that greater clearness and power, to say nothing of happiness of mind, can be exhibited in disease than in health, or else mankind should be supremely happy, as they happen to be more diseased than healthy. You may rest assured whatever devitalizes the brain and impairs the vigor or tone of organization, lowers the tone, lessens the grip, and dulls the perceptions, and modifies in proportion the manifestations of mind. In more serious proportions is the mind affected or destroyed as the physical defects of body and brain become greater or more permanent. Some may esteem this rank materialism ; I but see in it greater need for men to know themselves better, and to have some more regard for their bodies and brains than heretofore —" Honor God in their bodies," as well as " their souls, which are God's."

Health is essential to right-thinking and right (eous) actions. Great thoughts, noble sentiments, words that breathe and thoughts which burn, words of life and vigorous actions, are not the products of disease. Health is necessary to greatness. It is not to be denied that some have done wonders and achieved greatness under adverse circumstances; nevertheless, the principles I contend for are true, and in no way affected by apparent incidents of an opposite character. Health is largely a constitutional matter; it must be born in us. So there is something in blood after all. Nothing can be more important to the individual than to be born right, and after that keep right. You must make the hereditary and hygienic aspect of this subject your study, so that you may be the better adapted to help the fallen, and support or succour the weak; to train men and women in the way they should go.

Health, like character, manifests itself in structure, in form and appearance. The manly, virile step, action and build, the clear eye, pure skin, can be readily detected from the backboneless shuffle, the cod-fish eye, sallow skin and toothless pouches of the played-out *roué* and hypochondriac. Health and disease play an important part in character. Why is the bright and brilliant man of yesterday, then so clear-headed and prompt, so reliable and manly, now so sapless, withered and undone? Yesterday, the nerve currents flowed rhythmically, the bright arterial blood bounded on its appointed course, while the venous blood returned with healthy even flow to its destined haven. To-day, all this is altered, fell disease has done its work and has made all the differences we note in character. Outwardly, all of the man appears the same. In organic quality, temperament, size and form of body and head, there are no radical changes as yet: only the health spirit has fled. The breathing, circulatory, digestive and nutritive forces are altered. The temperature of the body has undergone a marked change. The activity and briskness, clear-headedness and force with which the character was marked are no longer there. The conditions of health, or rather absence of health, making all the difference, etc. This is an extreme illustration, but will serve my purpose. There are various degrees of health, from the buoyancy and soundness of youthful days, to the baleness which often accompanies good old age. It would be as impossible to describe the innumerable stages and degrees of health or disease, as it would be to describe the innumerable forms of head which a phrenologist in fair practice would handle in twelve months. In good health the flame of life burns normally; soundness of constitution is exhibited by *ease*, in the performance of all physical functions, such actions creating the highest degree of enjoyment. And within phrenological expression, activity, buoyancy, clear-headedness, pleasurable feelings and happiness resulting therefrom. The flame of life may burn low; may have been always feeble through inherited weakness or disease. The possessor of such debilitated constitution is ever feebly struggling for existence, life being made up of fitful gleams, and lingering hopes. Or the flame burns low, because of reckless expenditure and prodigality of life force, the condition of organization being but the natural outcome of a long train of devitalizing habits, which in themselves may have arisen out of abnormal mental or sensuous predilections,—or from some one or many of those accidental developments of self-gratification to which uninstructed human nature is somewhat prone. Improper diet, excess in eating and drinking, and insanitation will be found to lie at the root of nine-tenths of all human depravity reflected in this condition of health—or, rather, the want of it. Again, the flame of life may burn high, too high, strong and uncontrollable. Illicit passions and high burning fevers may bring a strong constitution low, and terminate the existence of a feeble one. In the first, life is the outcome of healthy, natural, or normal conditions. In the second, there is a lack of those conditions which make up healthy life. In the third, or last, there is the rapid and fiery consumption of life as exhibited in fevers, and other violent adjustments of the *vis medicatrix naturæ* to cast out disease and resume dominance in the organization. As a phrenological practitioner, you will meet with "the seven ages of man;" so will you meet with all conditions of life as affected by health and disease. It will be your duty to see how far character is affected by these conditions, and in what proportion, and by your advice—hygienic advice rather than medical—you will aid your patrons to return to the best conditions of life most in harmony with the laws of health.

Some individuals may be overflowing with life, buoyancy, and all the happiness which comes with it. It will be yours to teach them how to treasure what they have, how to preserve and maintain, how to utilize and direct the same into useful channels. Others may have less of this constitutional buoyancy and vigor, yet be sturdy and robust, able to manifest great physical power, endure labor, pain, and hardships with fortitude. Help these to cultivate their mental and moral powers, to preserve their health, that their powers of usefulness may be increased and prolonged. Others may have a fair degree of vital stamina; let them know the value of self-denial, temperance, of a calm and peaceful mind, so that they may avoid overwork and all extremes which exhaust nature, and hasten the premature termination of life. Others, again, may have but a fair degree of health, without buoyancy, sprightliness, or zeal—only sufficient to make them slow (if conscientious) workers, if so directed. Direct each according to character, health, ability, and the materials with which you have to work. Others may be tame and mechanical, without elasticity of step or brightness of soul, lacking in health without exhibiting any special form of disease. Search out the cause, whatever it be, bring it and your patient face to face.

It may be inherited, or the result of ignorance, or, it may be, of sin—that is, personal evil-doing. But, whatever the cause or causes, if you can help, let them not die from "lack of knowledge." Their restoration to health is the first parallel to be won. Mind cannot be great or clear which has to manifest itself through a brain enfeebled by disease, and through a body "scarce half-made up," and that of such stuff, imperfect nutrition, poor blood, and feeble nerves can make it.

Health is ease—ease the normal and natural action of every physical function in living things. Want of health, or ill-health is disease—discomfort in physical action. Frequently, the disease is but an effort of nature to restore the normal condition of ease, or health.

Health, then, is haleness, soundness, completeness, wholeness, wholesomeness, righteousness of the physical organization. In plants, animals, and man it is the basis of vigorous life. In man the basis of orderly and vigorous life—"a sound mind in a sound body." Ill-health or disease is naturally the complement of the above, and, therefore, the unnatural condition of plants, animals, or man, as constituted by the Supreme Being, and revealed to those who care to read God's laws as written within and without us—in the constitution of man and his environment.

Phrenology has to do with man—with mind, and therefore with the laws of health; but as there cannot be mind or (mental) laws of health without a physiological basis, it is important to the phrenologist that he should have such an insight—pathological, if you will—knowledge of that basis, so as to be the true "guide, philosopher, and friend" of those who shall consult him. Apart from such phrenological developments as tend to excitability, despondency, unevenness, excessive anxiety, defective hope, abnormal cautiousness, and what not, *Health* plays such an important part in man's disposition, ability, and character, no genuine advice can be given without taking these into consideration. It is your duty, and the duty of every phrenologist, to study human nature honestly as a whole; to study those laws of life, being, health, hygiene and sanitation, and apply them to the welfare of himself and others who may consult him. Let the phrenologist *magnify his office* by earnestly, anxiously, and truthfully striking at the evils which underlie and undermine health and character—whatever their source—within or without the individual. If at all preventable and removable causes, let him labor for their removal. Preventive hygiene or medicine is hardly yet within the sphere of medical practice and responsibility. The medical man is, as a rule, called in to prescribe and cure, not to advise and educate the people, and prevent disease; much less to give instruction in the art of living, in the formation of right habits, or the perfection of character, or in the choice of pursuits. It is the phrenologist who does this; and in doing so he cannot interfere with the medical profession or practice,—save on the broad and higher grounds of the prevention of disease, and the physical, mental, and moral improvement of the individual and the community.

PATHOLOGICAL PHYSIOGNOMY.

When you are estimating the influence of health and disease as affecting character, the physiology of the individual, as presented by his or her temperament, will be found important. Each temperament, according to its predominance, will have its own characteristic derangements, concerning which the possessor of the temperament should ever be on his guard. PATHOLOGICAL PHYSIOGNOMY might with advantage be elevated to the dignity of a professorship and a chair in our medical schools. As it is, it cannot escape the attention of the observant medico-physiologist, or o b s e r v a n t phrenologist, that disease as well as temperament have their characteristic features or physiognomy by which they can be diagnosed or detected.

A description of the various temperamental conditions is not intended now; later on I shall briefly describe them. Each temperamental condition has its own peculiar innate or family derangements—such as mental and nervous diseases with the mental temperament, diseases of the nutritive and digestive viscera with the vital temperament, rheumatic and muscular diseases with the motive temperament. The vital predisposes to short or acute diseases, inflammatory in character; the motive to slow and chronic derangements or diseases; the combina-

tions of the temperament to various complications. With one person acute bronchitis shortens the career; while with another chronic and distressing asthma hold its sway, but seems to have no appreciable effect on the longevity of the individual. Consumption of the lungs may exist with mental clearness, nervous excitation, and delusive hopes—but not with mental robustness. No condition of *disease* can be favorable to mental greatness, usefulness, and holiness.

The more perfect our physical and mental conditions, the more perfectly are we adapted for their manifestation. Sickness may bring reflection, thoughtfulness, but I doubt if it ever brought either great goodness or usefulness. The Abrahams, Noahs, Elijahs, Johns, Peters, and Luthers, the Joshuas, Maccabes, Cæsars, Washingtons, Wellingtons, Lincolns, and Grants, were not creatures that would be sickly saints if they could, but rather valiant soldiers, healthy men, whose features bore the impress of manliness as well as goodness.

Sickness, disease, and death, I admit, have their uses in the order of nature, creation, and Divine government, or else they would not be. We live because others have died; and we will live and die to repeat the tale. It has taken generations of deaths to fit this world for man; while, stranger still, his death has contributed to his advancement—*i. e.*, mankind. Nevertheless, it is not sickly souls in rheumatic carcasses who move the masses, lead, guide, and control the world, it is rather those who in the full possession of all their powers, have been able to do so.

The deceased, sickly, or broken down, are rather examples of violated law, non-servitude to the Creator's will or Nature's laws. Say what you will, our best life will be our truest life; and our best and truest life can only be the outcome of our healthiest and purest conditions.

In times past or present, the wine of inspiration has not been poured into old bottles or broken flasks, but always into receptacles worthy *or filled for it.* Look high up or look down, search and see, where has there been one sickly lantern-jawed dyspeptic who done ought for his day and generation worthy of the name, which might not have been much better accomplished when in the full possession (by health) of his faculties? I can point to the many **who have** stamped on those about **them** the robustness of their goodness, and the whole-heartedness of their nature, by the mighty magnetism of love and true earnestness of purpose. Decrepitude and disease can only produce kindred fruit. The signs of health and disease are not hard to read. Vitativeness and longevity are never found with ears buried in the head, or with a weak and retreating chin; good digestion and corresponding nutritive energy with a hollow cheek and high cheek bones; vitality with a sunken and leaden expression; robust lungs with small nostrils and thin and weak muscles; vigorous circulation with a pale or yellow skin, cold feet and hands. Persons hollow beneath the eyes are predisposed to consumption, while those who are **full** there are strong in lung and sound in wind and limb, etc.

Health and longevity are dependent on organization or constitution, good habits and good surroundings, organism and environment, but principally on organization.

The physician who is not a phrenologist, is necessarily at greater disadvantage in diagnosing disease than one who is both. A phrenologist is less called upon to treat disease than he is called to point out where character, talent, ability, etc., are affected, modified, or undermined by it. It is therefore of importance to you to know whether the brain is supplied by healthy or diseased blood; whether the mental and the physical powers are working in harmony, or opposed to each other, and in what degree; whether the mental powers are strained, in what sense and by what cause or causes; all this is important to you. It is for you to read character through its physical basis of soundness or otherwise. *Behind* the bright eye, (fringed by long eyelashes), delicate nostrils, and soft and tender skin, pretty heightened color, and fulness at centre of each cheek—the face of beauty, with all the vivacity and fickleness of manner—you may detect phthisis or deadly consumption. In fulness of flesh, bright complexion, and somewhat thick upper lip, you may detect scrofula. In pasty, dingy complexions; kidney disease. In waxy appearances and bloodless features; uterine affections. In the ogling glance and restless **eye;** the *persist-*

ence of amatory *inconsistency* and local brain disease. In the persistent smiling, staring, stupid and idiotic grin, brain affections. In restlessness and anxiety, depression of spirits, organic nervous derangement of heart and lungs. In the loose-hanging jaw, *ennui*, want of spirit, ambition and pluck, stomachic derangements, poor digestion, mesenteric diseases; flushing in the face with blueness under the eyes in children, teething, worms, and menstrual troubles; and in men and women pneumonia, nervous exhaustion and weakness. In the constant red face, gouty tendencies, inflammatory difficulties, and fondness of stimulants. The face bloated and blotched with red nose; drunkenness or high living and imperfect circulation. Red cheeks with paleness about the mouth and nose, sunken under the eyes, worms, and intestinal difficulties. With the wrinkled face, old age; in children, imperfect nutrition and precocity; in half-grown lads and men, immoral habits, self-abuse, and venery. Yellow complexion, with white of the eyes tinged with yellow, torpid liver, inactivity, sedentary habits, and so on. I lay down no general law for you, so much depends upon skill and practice. It is true (in phrenology) you are not required to administer medicine, practice midwifery or surgery. Your work is to analyze character, to detect defects therein and expose them with a view to their successful eradication or cure, whatever they may be—evil habits, that they may be given up, secret transgressions against light and knowledge, so that by their exposure

they may fade away like ancient mummies before the light of the sun and exposure to air. To discover latent talent, to direct manhood's gifts into the most useful and noble channels, and to help your fellow man in all honest ways to a true knowledge of himself. Where you find man's ignorance of self stand in his way of advancement, it is your duty to enlighten him according to your ability, to understand and appreciate your offices; therefore the importance you, as a phrenologist, must attach to health, and the desire which you should possess, to see that all who consult you should maintain and foster such health as they have, and live in the full use of their powers, physical, mental, and moral, and in the abuse of none.

"That tone of mind depends upon vigor of organization" cannot be too often borne in mind, or repeated as a phrenological and physiological axiom; defective vigor in the one means defective tone in the other. Defective health means, then, less vigor and tone than would be possible under a normal condition of health.

MEMORY.

By health, the best foundation of memory can be laid. As health is essential to the growth, vigor, and robustness of all our faculties, it follows that with an impaired nervous system and a depleted brain, memory will be less tenacious and reliable than when the organization is unimpaired and the brain sound and vigorous. No matter how perfect the brain, even though the possessor is in a fair state of health, a heavy dinner an unusual glass of spirits, an exhausting walk, a sleepless night, a slight cold, are often sufficient to impair memory and interfere with normal brain action. How much more likely are the mental powers—memory—liable to be affected when the brain is depleted by disease, or when the course of life-work, morals —or the want of them—have been making unseen but steadfast drain upon the vitality? You will sometimes observe that the undue action of certain organs—say, of the social or selfish group — have effectually drained the knowing and reflective organs of all reliability of action in early life, which, later on, should be only the product of senility. Facts and incidents of twenty years ago, impinged upon the brain when mobile and active, and all the faculties more capable of photographing vivid impressions, will be remembered by some persons quite readily, when the facts and incidents of twenty weeks ago— twenty hours ago—are forgotten; forgotten, owing to the lack of vitality, and therefore less impressionability of the brain to receive impressions.

Health is essential to *memory.* The kind of memory will depend upon the brain formation. A child with small "form" and "imitation" will have some difficulty to remember and reproduce copy, or writing and drawing exercises, than another with the same quality and health of brain, but more favorably endowed with these faculties. Boys with a talent for figures will be better endowed with a good memory for figures than other lads wanting in

"calculation" and "causality." Persons who have no brains to appreciate facts will be poorly impressed with them, and consequently have a poor memory for them and so on. It must not be forgotten whatever the characteristic memory—mind powers—present, retrospective and active, *the memory will be exalted by health and deteriorated by disease.*

There are many persons who complain of their memory, when the fact really is that for some things only their memory is bad—some only ; and as often as not, it is not until the phrenological practitioner has clearly pointed out the special area of the defect in memory, that they become truly acquainted with their mental condition in this respect. Phrenology ascertains and points out in what particular memory is defective, and the cause or causes of the defect : deficient brain formation, deficient exercise of the faculty complained of—such as defective education or imperfect interest ; lack of brain vitality, imperfect health, and the cause of the imperfect health ; to any of these, or all combined, may be traced the defect in memory complained of. The phrenologist is called upon to advise the best steps to be taken for *the renewal of the mind* to its early vigor, presence, and power, or to such improvement as may be radically possible. Herein your knowledge of character and of hygiene can be applied with true advantage.

Health and memory are again intimately associated with the right exercise of the self-preservative organs. The self-preservative organs, left to themselves, are but " blind leaders of the blind." " Alimentiveness " simply gives the desire for, and is gratified by, eating and drinking ; but lacks discriminating knowledge, is not enabled to distinguish between the good and the bad, merely selecting that which gratifies the appetite most. It may long for and eat forbidden fruit and die. It may eat from mere necessity from the edible clays of South America to the street garbage of our cities and towns—but not from knowledge. " Alimentiveness " must be educated. " Vitativeness " gives love of life, creates an instinctive desire to live and preserve life ; but how, depends upon whether it is guided by " a Voice from Heaven " reaching it from above through the moral and intellectual organs, or from " below," tempting it to revel in sensuous enjoyment with " alimentiveness," " to eat, drink and be merry ; " or with perverted " amativeness " " to waste its substance with harlots ; " or in lesser follies, esteeming such gratification as the highest *acme* of human happiness—*i.e.*, its gratification. Courage, (combativeness) may just as readily defend " vitativeness," as to give it daring to go to extremes. Courage, without the restraining influences of conscience and caution, has often led " vitativeness " to " see life," " go out into the world," and through a " carnival of fun " terminate existence in the dance of death. " Executiveness," destructiveness, may destroy to find food to sustain life ; " acquisitiveness," to store it ; and " secretiveness " to secure it ; or " love of wom-

an " to prodigality, waste, and extravagance. For the unguided dominion of these propensities to lead their gratification pure and simple, without regard to the wisdom or the folly of the act, providing the act gives pleasure to the actor. The mental and moral faculties may be misused, but it is the abuse of the propensities, wilfully or ignorantly, which lies at the base of three-fourths of the ills which humanity are heir to. If the improper use, or abuse, of any of the faculties of mind, or organs of the brain, lead to the undermining of the health—to loss of memory, to the destruction of character—it is the phrenologist's duty to become a true preacher of " righteousness, temperance, and judgment " to those who seek his counsel. The reciprocal action of health and character are interblended, and never can in this life at least be disassociated. Every phrenologist worthy of the name studies physiology, the laws of health, the principles of hygiene, personal and domestic sanitation. He is not trespassing on the province of the medical practitioner. Thus, in so preparing yourself for your work as a phrenologist without such study and observation, your ability to discern and analyze character will be limited ; not only so, but you will fail to give suitable advice in circumstances where your advice would be most necessary and most surely appreciated.

APPLIED PHRENOLOGY.— FOURTH LECTURE.

In the preceding addresses, I have considered some health conditions, as affecting memory and character, and have endeavored briefly to point out some of the physical or physiognomical signs indicating the same. In this address, I shall briefly review the temperaments, and other conditions, which are essential to duly consider in reading character, and conclude with a hint or two on conduct in the consulting room. Next in importance of modifying or qualifying influences are the temperaments. For the sake of clearness and brevity, phrenologists wisely take for their bases of temperaments the natural physiological bases of the organization in health, and not the pathological and physiological classification of the medical schools. By the term temperament, we understand that condition or state of body depending upon the relative energy of its various functions. As a matter of fact, there are as many temperaments as there are functions in the organization, but they are all subordinate to the three grand temperaments, or physiological systems into which the organization is divided; viz., the nutritive or vital temperament, the mechanical or motive temperament, the nervous or mental temperament.

The vital temperament is, then, based on the nutritive system, i. e., the lungs, stomach, blood, and lymphatic organic nervous system, the office of which is to elaborate life or vitality. It is presented in two prominent forms: First—in greater width and depth of the cavity of the thorax or chest, than of the abdominal region. Hence the greater activity of the arterial system, the lungs and capillary vessels being most prominent. The eyes are blue or grey; hair, light brown, auburn, or red; complexion of "good color"—bright or florid. The individual in general character is noted for warmth, enthusiasm, geniality, fondness for life, good company, "goodness of heart," and pleasant social surroundings. It is the money-making temperament, makes the most of everything—ease, comfort, generosity, domesticity, etc. Second—form of the temperament presents greater fulness of the abdominal region than of the chest and thorax, greater activity of the lymphatic system than in the foregoing, less arterial activity, slowness in breathing, (nature requiring greater mental and physical stimuli to arouse it), paleness of skin, and, in some instances, presenting general flabbiness; hair light to dark. Vitality is manufactured faster than there is activity, mental or physical, to work it off. This is the grease-making organization, and is often accompanied by a character in which laziness and selfishness are personified. To lounge, sit, eat, drink, smoke, and gratify the sensuous nature generally, as opposed to mental and moral greatness, is characteristic. Then there is the lymphatic, bilious form of this temperament, which gives a pendulous abdomen—a Falstaffian corporation of unusual proportions, so dear to "City Alderman," "Poor-law Guardians," and such retired respectability as indulges in sumptuous feasts and wine banquets at other peoples' expense. The lymphatic and bilious form of this temperament are abnormal or diseased physiological conditions of the organization. Mental langor and debility, sluggish circulation, with its innumerable diseases, stomachic derangements, dropsy, tumors, scrofula, bad legs, bad heart, and a bad liver, are some of its fruits. Yet what else can be expected than that a man should have a bad liver who has a bad heart, and who daily violates the good laws of nature, instead of learning that obedience which brings destined happiness in its train?

The motive temperament is based on the mechanical system, the tentpoles and ropes of our earthly tabernacle, our framework of bones, and muscles, and ligaments. This temperament presents itself in two forms —the dark or bilious, the light or sanguine, in proportion as the lungs, heart, liver, stomach, etc., are influential in the organization. This is the temperament of manliness, industry, energy, determination, self-reliance, muscular power, and physical endurance. Character in this, as in the foregoing or vital temperament, will be powerfully influenced by its predominance. As stated elsewhere, the brain formation will correspond with the dominating temperament.

The mental temperament is based upon the brain, spinal cord, and nervous system; motor, sensory and sympathetic. This is the temperament of "I think," as the vital is of "I live and I enjoy," or the motive of "I work and execute." It is the temperament of progress and culture. Its excess is the curse of civilization; its want, the

characteristic of barbarism. It is needless to say there can be no sensitiveness of feeling, keenness of enjoyment, susceptibility of suffering or capacity for enjoyment, mental or moral progress or greatness, without the existence of this temperament. Character corresponds to its influence. The size and form of the head indicate its presence by the fulness of the perceptive, knowing, intellectual, intuitional, spiritual, and semi-refining faculties.

The vital temperament includes the breathing, circulatory, and digestive powers, and is affected by the natural or healthy, abnormal or diseased, condition of the organs manifesting these functions, the character corresponding. The mental temperament is characterized by a head relatively large, and a comparatively small, neat body. The features of the face are delicately moulded, fineness throughout manifested; voice, clear, silvery, and flexible. It is the temperament of refinement. The figure is graceful or elegant, rather than robust or commanding. Activity, clearheadedness, and excitability or susceptibility to impressions, are characteristics. Nothing is so desirable as a healthy condition of this temperament; nothing so undesirable as the reverse. The finer the organization, the more liable it is to derangement.

In animal life and processes the vital is creative—broods, breeds, and sustains; the motive executes, builds, engineers, and pioneers; the mental originates, perceives, reflects, and refines. All are interlinked, and combine their forces for good or ill, according to the quality of the organization and brain capacity, size, and shape.

Activity of organization is indicated by litheness, slenderness in men as in animals—race-horse, greyhound, and antelope are examples. **Excitability** by sharpness; sharp features, pointed noses and chins, thin straight lips, are **signs.** Thin straight lips are not desirable; although they may indicate cuteness, penetration, they are seldom accompanied by coolness of judgment, patience, or affection.

That character is influenced by predominence of temperament is undoubted. It is desirable to have a balance of temperament in harmonious proportion to have a harmonious character. Where the mental temperament is dominant, there may be intellectual brilliancy, at the lack of general **strength** or force. Where the vital predominates there may be love of ease, comfort, life, and present gratification, at the cost of moral and intellectual growth and spirituality. The motive **temperament** in excess would give slowness, ruggedness, and angularity to character. Where the temperaments are more **harmoniously** blended—the motive, **giving** endurance; the vital, ardor; the mental, intelligence and spirituality;—we find health, **vigor,** long life, great usefulness and goodness as the outcome of such completeness and full-orbing of the organization.

Organic quality is that **quality of** organization which is innate, inbred— the quality of our breeding, good or bad, which comes with ourselves into this life. It underlies all temperament. It gives **fineness** to the motive, and makes a Gladstone of one who might otherwise have been a coal-heaver. It gives purity to the vital, and makes a Spurgeon of one who might have been a tapster or brewer's vanman. It refines the mental, and tends to goodness of soul and life, as it gives grain, fineness of grain or fibre to the organization. It is more easily perceived, detected, than described, beyond the information already recorded in our textbooks. It is the mystic power pervading our being which proclaims our lineage, and gives tone, bias, and intensity to our entire nature—mental and physical. It is not a polished coin, but the purity of the metal of which the coin is made. It is not the airs and mannerisms of my lady, or lady's lady, the etiquette of ballrooms or the tricks and jargon of this set or of that society. It is inbred perfection, congenital and hereditary, and is indicated by the general harmony of form, texture of skin, fineness of hair, delicacy (not unhealthiness) and refinement of structure throughout.

CONSULTATIONS.

In giving consultations the professional phrenologist will, as a rule, be more frequently consulted by women than by men. Woman has naturally more curiosity than man; her own natural intuitions lead her in the direction of phrenology. She knows her little ones best, is spent, and spends hours with them that is not possible to man. On her is largely thrown the burden of moulding the characters of her children. Nevertheless, notwithstanding her intimate knowledge of the children, she finds much to perplex, much to explain, and in phrenology finds just the information she most needs. Woman is more observant and intuitive than man : she feels, and sees, and arrives at the truth of things, and gets at the heart of her little circle, concerning which man has done but little except to touch the outward fringe. She feels, he reasons. Woman has greater love for children as a rule than man, and is more likely than he to consult the phrenologist when she finds her own judgment at fault as to the best steps to take for her children's welfare, their management, how to train them, what process of education will be best to remedy their defects and fit them for the work of life, how overcome or counterbalance hereditary defects, develop the moral and religious nature and strengthen the mental, ascertain what their special calling should be, and how best to fit them for it. Here, again, in the exercise of your profession as a phrenologist you will find you have not entered upon a sinecure. The future usefulness and happiness of these little ones are in a measure in your hands. When possible it is advisable that a phrenological examination should be made of both parents. It will materially help you to a fuller insight into the children's characters. It will do more, for, from the confidence which is created by a careful examination of the parents, will give all the more diligence to carry out your advice given on behalf of their children. By the

examination of the parents as well as of the children, you will see how far the boys partake of the mother's constitution and disposition, the girls the father's, or wherein the children approximate to the character of either parent. What are the weaknesses and eccentricities in the children, and in what sense they are inherited, intensified, or modified. The knowledge thus gained is invaluable ; invaluable alike to the phrenologist, parents, and the children. The husband and wife may not understand one another as they should. Their individualities and dispositions may clash rather than blend. They neither bear nor forbear. A phrenological examination will enable them to realize where they are most likely to be inharmonious, and what steps they must take if they would live well and do well together, and have their children well brought up by the greater influence of example supporting precept. What is more important still, that their unborn children might not inherit their "jars" and "cranks." You will have to advise young people how to make judicious marriages. Such marriages, to be harmonious and lasting, must be predicated on the approximation of moral and mental natures, harmony in tastes and pursuits, similarity of position, means and religious views, otherwise they may be slightly contrasted in organization and temperament. The mental temperament, seeking more fibre and vitality for the offspring by marriage with one who has these characteristics in a larger degree. All extremes and positive contrasts should be avoided. An "orderly" man and a "disorderly" woman, can never be happy. A "saving" woman and a "thoughtless" man, would make a bad pulling team for life. Where the parties are likely to dovetail in the major points of constitution, health, disposition and tastes, the union will become as conjugally complete in time as the ossification of the frontal bone in the skulls of most people.

Great judgment is required to give a calm and impartial decision in a matter like this. When you, as the examiner, are sure of the character of each, you should in the discharge of your duty put all points of agreement and disagreement before your clients, leaving with them the responsibility of acting according to your advice. In this, as in other matters, I only make suggestions here. Their practical application must depend upon the experience and ability which you will have to apprehend the natures and dispositions of those who call upon you, and your client's power to apply the advice given.

In the examinations of the heads of men and women it will be found, as a rule, men possess characteristics purely masculine, the woman those which are feminine. It has been observed in some instances that the female possesses certain masculine traits, and some men the feminine; but whether male or female, the character will always correspond with the organization and cranial development of each. The average size of a woman's head is smaller than that of man. So is her body smaller than that of man. In many instances it will be found that her head is relatively larger in proportion to her body than that of man. Also that woman's organization is the finer, as well as possessing a greater proportion of brain and nervous development to the size of the body, than in the case of her lord and master. There is a vulgar idea abroad that woman is inferior to man: this is a gross error. She may be, and is, inferior to man physically in some respects, and is thereby unfitted to do a man's work, or fulfil the duties of a man in his special province in life. It is not intended, however, that she should do man's work, any more than man should do her work and fill her position in life. Nevertheless, woman can run man very close, and beat him in most pursuits in life. In fact, there is but little man can do which a woman could not do better, except being a father. She can manage an estate, be a banker or a bill-broker, navigate a ship, prove a true physician, and is the only true nurse; as in physics so in law, divinity, and learning she has proved herself man's compeer. In the true spirit of courage, devotion, and hero(ine)ism she has proved herself man's equal. Of course there are two sides to this as to all other questions. Woman is only inferior to man in matters purely masculine, as man is inferior to woman in matters purely feminine. What a poor hand a man makes at womanly work and womanly duties if left to himself! Yet how indignant he would be, if, in consequence, he was perpetually informed he was inferior to woman. Is it not true that, woman being physically incapable of doing man's work, she is esteemed to be his inferior?

Men and women have their respective spheres in nature, the boundary lines of which they cannot cross, any more than the Ethiopian can change his skin or the leopard his spots. They are essential to each other, the complements of each other, helpmates to one another, but in no sense inferior to each other. It amuses me to see a paper-collar nonentity selling stays and tape, pins and laces to a woman, calling himself a man, and declare that the sex which produced the mother of Christ, and Elizabeth Fry, a Grace Darling, a Florence Nightingale, a noble-souled sister Dora, and gentle loving mothers and sisters innumerable, with and without fame, are inferior creatures to him, because they don't swagger, smoke cigarettes, take B.-and-S., and otherwise conduct themselves as these "lords of creation" do, whose opinions of woman are formed by the companionship, which they most desire to keep.

As there are physical differences, so there are mental differences which distinguish the sex. Men are distinguished by certain mental and physical characteristics which are purely masculine and not possessed by woman; women are distinguished by certain mental and physical characteristics which men do not possess. Each have their own sphere of life and action. The weakness or inferiority of either must hinge on the answer to the question, Which of the two sexes most faithfully and admirably discharge the duties of their allotted spheres? Whoever reads may answer Is intuition, delicacy, tenderness, purity, order, love of offspring, educatibility, obedience, respect for authority, love of the true and beautiful, the superior prerogative of man's or woman's nature? Has woman ever had the encouragement, kindly treatment, educational advantages accorded to man? Where she has had such advantages has she not held her own percentage for percentage, equalled the qualifications and successes of men? She may not dig and build, invent and construct with man, for by organization and divine law he is to till the soil and she is to mother and bring up his family; she is to instil her sweetness and purity into the minds of his—not his, but their—combined offspring. As a woman she is stronger in many characteristics than man, who is as a man stronger in many characteristics than the woman. That is all; who then is the weakest? Who shall answer? God grant that each man may learn to fulfil his allotted sphere as creditably and as truly as woman has shown herself capable of doing. Who is inferior? Who shall answer? It is an idle question; the outcome of animal strength, brute force, and the physical dominance of man—the creature of his stronger passions and physical strength, not of his better self, which finds in woman his other half, nor in or from Him who from the beginning made them to be one.

IN THE CONSULTING ROOM.

Receive visitors courteously; hand

them your fee list; take the names and addresses of all who consult you; add thereto nature of consultation and amount of fee paid. Place person to be examined in a comfortable chair; carefully note to the best of your ability general appearance, health, temperament, and organic quality. Then measure the head, manipulate, and proceed to describe character. If time admit of it, the head can be described by groups of organs—from the crown of the head for will, purpose, resolution, application, or the want of these characteristics; from the side head for hold upon life, executiveness, energy, and courage, or otherwise; from the back head for domesticity, conjugality, love of home, children, sociability, affection, attachment, etc.; from the perceptives for the bases they give to character, how they see what their possessor most desires to see, capacity for localizing, individualizing, detecting, and discriminating; the literary faculties, the pursuit of knowledge, how used or neglected, particular memory and general memory, means of cultivation, etc., the effect of health, etc., and so on, until the moral and religious and semi-refining faculties are included in your researches. Each group, according to size and position, describe to the best of your judgment, the most prominent, and therefore the most influential, group first. There is nothing like making a good hit at the beginning. It opens the mind of your patron to listen attentively, and to secure his or her attention to your subsequent advice. The examination can be closed by a *resumé* of the whole,

briefly pointing out the leading characteristics, strength or weakness, of the person examined,—making allowances for such combinations which seem necessary. The phrenologist should not joke, nor be familiar at any time with patrons. At the same time he should be kindly, sage, sober-minded, and quietly uphold the dignity and power of phrenology as a science by his discrimination, thoughtfulness, manner and appearance.

The phrenologist, like the medical practitioner, should charge fees according to the position he has attained in the profession. It is, however, best to be moderate at the beginning of career, viz.: 2s. 6d. for a verbal consultation; 5s. for the same, with brief written statement of character or chart; 10s. 6d. or £1 1s. for full written statements, according to time occupied, and the size of the written analysis of character. If necessary, one day a week might be set aside, when a short verbal statement might be given at reduced fees.

The consulting room should be centrally located, in a self-advertising position. It should always be neat and orderly, supplied with a selected stock of literature on phrenology, physiology, and health; with hygienic appliances, such as Indian clubs, dumb-bells, health lifts, chest expanders, etc. By keeping good and useful books a correct knowledge of phrenology is disseminated, and suitable books should be presented to the notice and sold to patrons and patients after consultation, which may be deemed most useful for them.

PHRENOLOGICAL QUERIES AND ANSWERS.

FIFTH LECTURE.

SOME of these queries have naturally arisen in the minds of phrenological beginners when attempting to apply phrenology to practice, and have been put to me by pupils in their anxiety to get at practical results. I give them and the answers here by way of an appendix to "Applied Phrenology."

1ST QUERY.

Persons generally come to phrenologists to test the science.. They are not willing, as a rule, to give any kind of information to the phrenologist, lest in so doing, they may afford the examiner some clue to their character. Now, as education necessarily exerts a powerful influence over character, how can its influence be determined : from organization, temperament, or sharpness —pointedness—in the development of the phrenological organs, etc. ?

ANSWER.

Those who treat a phrenologist in the above manner, simply exhibit ignorance of the nature and character of the science whose teachers or exponents they are about to consult. They also exhibit their own shallowness— self-satisfaction—in a very readable manner. Most people when consulting a physician, or a solicitor—seeking medical or legal advice—generally give all the information (from their point of view) they can to their adviser. In doing so, they think they are acting best in their own interests. Phrenological clients would best consult their own interests if they would act in the same reasonable manner. If a parent would know for what his boy was best adapted, he would do well to inform the phrenologist what are his own views on the matter ; also volunteer information as to the boy's education and inclination for certain pursuits (if any). He might also with advantage inform the examiner about the classses of employments, business pursuits, and professions in his own neighborhood, and possible influence of himself and friends in obtaining an entrance for his child into one or other of them. Two things— the boy's education and the parents' influence as to selection of pursuit— will be important factors, in addition to the youth's proclivities and character, in enabling the conscientious practitioner in arriving at a decision.

Education is not something added to the character distinct from itself. It is rather the innate qualities educed or drawn out, improved upon or otherwise by a certain course of discipline, and the natural growth in civilization of the various faculties under the stimulus of the senses themselves, automatic or otherwise. Education is in general a storing of the mind by the cultivation of memory—a process of creating striking or vivid impressions —which are to some extent afterward retained, and can be automatically and consciously reproduced. "Language" (in memory and expression) is drawn out, exercised or cultivated. The faculties of observation are appealed to, and their attention directed to certain objects—organic or inorganic—in the world without. "Calculation," "eventuality," "comparison," and "causality," "time," "tune," and "constructiveness" are in time brought into play. A certain amount of discipline is also exercised on the moral, social and selfish nature, generally through "approbativeness" and "acquisitiveness," etc. Perhaps the most powerful agents of education are those forces of example and association, whether in school or out of it, which affect the majority through "imitation."

In any case, a person can only be educated according to organization and cranial development. Such qualities as the person may have can be called out, exercised to their fullest, or perverted to their lowest, according to the character of the education. Education neither adds to, nor conceals anything from, the knowledge of the practical phrenologist which may not be practically detected in the course of consultation. Whatever the influence or effect of the education, unless most recent, it must be seen in the permanent results produced in organization and character.

Education or discipline has a modifying influence on innate capacity—character—or else the phrenological advice to "restrain" or "cultivate" would be meaningless terms.

The stock-raiser and horse-trainer would not pay so much attention to breeding and "breaking in," had he not already certain good materials to work upon. What is this "breaking in" but education—the directing of the qualities or faculties the horse already possesses, so as to make him more serviceable to man. No "breaking in" will give breed, stamina, spirit, nerve, fineness of fibre, if not already inherent. True, lack of training or education will deteriorate these qualities somewhat. No amount of education can give capacity where it is not possessed, neither can it change inbred grain or quality. It cannot change a cart-horse into a race-horse. Although this "breaking in," training, education, what not, with its right feeding, good brushing, fair work, and kindness in treatment, may make the horse brighter, more healthy and useful, yet, when all is done, the cart-horse will still be no more than a cart-horse, the race-horse a race-horse. Neither can education change the Ethiopian into a Caucasian, nor either of them into aught else than what their present organization and phrenological development declare them capable of being.

The uneducated waif will be distinguished by his appearance from the refined and cultured youth, and each from each other, by the individuality of their organization and cranial development, rather than by the scholastic attainments of the one, and the utter lack of these in the other. So you may know the true character of either, as you would distinguish a drunken man from a sober one—not by what he assumes to be, or by what he hides, but by what he really is.

If the organization is fine, "the organs of educatibility"—the observing, literary, reasoning, and intuitive faculties—favorably developed, "conscientiousness," "acquisitiveness," "constructiveness,"" continuity," with the semi-refining and aspiring faculties sufficiently influential, you can pronounce with certainty as to the influence of education. If certain organs are more fully developed than others, "locality" or "causality," for instance, should they present sharpness or pointedness, it will indicate that their development has been more recent than that of other organs. Roundness, fulness, and smoothness are generally indicative of normal growth. Exercise your judgment upon careful examination.

I understand, generally speaking, education to mean primary, secondary, and higher class scholastic training, which is obtainable at our private and public schools, academies, colleges, and universities throughout the country; but whether in this sense, or in a broader one, my answer is sufficiently full for practical purposes. I may add that, in girls under 11, and boys under 14, years of age, the influence of education in the foregoing sense will be quite appreciable in cranial formation as well as in that "lighting up" of the physiognomy which distinguishes the apt lad from the dullard. The influence of education at school, and its further development by trade, occupation, pursuit, and habit, is more detectable in woman and in man than in childhood. The phrenological development, build, physiognomical expression of head and face are then more definite. Educational

influences—i. e., scholastic training— are most marked in those organizations which are fine in quality, full in the frontal cerebral lobes, where the mental temperament, in some of its forms presents itself. In a word, where there are brains to educate, they can be educated; and, if educated, the influence, and presence of such influence, are discernible in "contour and quality," and readily interpreted by the phrenologist.

In practice, skilful observation of head and face, mannerism, ease, grace, correctness or otherwise of speech, are all worthy of consideration in estimating the influence of education. Such indications are not to be despised, even if their observation savor of commonplace. The influence of education is, therefore, discernible in organization, phrenological development, physiognomy, and manners.

2ND QUERY.

In taking the measurement of the head, how should a chart be marked, if the measurement one way is not in proportion to measurements another way? You say, "The average size of the male head is 22 inches in circumference, with length and coronal height about 14½ inches. This size I should mark in register 4, or average 22½, with corresponding length and height. I should mark 5, or full." But suppose there is not "corresponding length and height," how do you manage then? Do you make allowances for these differences in marking the register, or no?

ANSWER

Yes, always! Marking charts, in my private opinion, as far as the public are concerned, is comparatively of little scientific value. You can only at best mark that which approximates to your conception of the truth, as no two heads are exactly alike; the marking of certain stereotyped phrases (however good and explanatory) can never be satisfactory It is useful simply as an aid to the memory of the person whose head has been examined, and to the phrenologist, in that it takes far less time to mark than it would to write a careful and accurate analysis of character.

When marking your chart take into consideration, as much as possible, "future conditions" as well "as present development," and mark to encourage development of character, so that each trait, strength or weakness, may stand out clear to the person's mind who seeks your phrenological aid. Be particular to show clearly what you want cultivated or restrained, in order to perfect character within the limits of the possible capacity of the individual.

Where it can be done, always advise your patrons to have a written statement. Recommend it not only as an aid to their memory, but as being less liable to misinterpretation and contradictory statements than the markings on a chart sometimes suggest. Your aim in marking a chart is to give as accurate a delineation of character as the circumstances will admit. Absolute correctness in every particular is not claimed, neither is it possible, and short of a written statement, due allowance, in every case, must be made to the examiner and the examined. It is well to accustom yourself to writing "Summaries of Character," and "Full written Analysis of Character." As I have hinted elsewhere, write as you would speak ; use no physiological, anatomical and phrenological technicalities which can be avoided. Remember, you write to give information and help—help to aid the boy to be a man, the man to be the better man, and both how to occupy their truest and best sphere in life with honor and credit to themselves.

In conclusion, as to these chart markings, write down whatever you consider is truest to the character of the person examined. Remember, you are dealing with "variable quantities" and not "mathematical certainties." When you find $4\frac{1}{2}$ fails to express your meaning, and 5 does, use 5. Thus a 22 inch brain, with 5 or 6 in quality, 5 or 6 in activity and excitability, standing 6 mental, 5 vital, and 5 motive temperaments, if 4 or average, as applied to size of brain, does not (for instance with L. N. Fowler's Self-instructor) fully represent its power, write 5 if that would be the truest approximation. It is, however, best not to suppose cases; when actual ones come before you, act according to your best judgment. You cannot do better

Written and purely verbal descriptions of character are best. Marked charts and registers have done more to bring phrenology into disrepute than anything else I know of, save the downright ignorance of the whole science exhibited by those so-called "professors" and perambulating phrenological quacks who so much discredit phrenology throughout the country.

3RD QUERY.

Excitability and activity :—Is sharpness of features and form, an unfailing measure of excitability, or length of features, of activity ?

ANSWER.

No, to the former part of this question ; yes, as a rule, to the latter. Excitability, intense susceptibility, or sensitiveness, with or without health, is one of the conditions found in connection with a fine or delicate organization having a predominance of brain and nerve, as in the mental temperament. Activity, sprightliness, and vivacity, are more frequently indicated by a healthy vital-mental, mental-vital, and mental-motive organization, than by any other temperamental combination. In the sense that a greyhound is more active than a bull-dog, a race-horse than a cart-horse, length or slimness indicates activity. Nevertheless, persons can be tall and slim and *heart-lazy.* Little people, as a rule, are more active than big folk, for the reason that the nerve currents travel more rapidly in small and fine organizations than in large and coarse ones.

4TH QUERY.

What is your opinion of the use of calipers, phreno-physiometers, and of mathematical measurements such as suggested by Stratton, as aids in arriving at character ?

ANSWER.

All of these are valuable enough with certain gentlemen who delight in the pedantry of phrenology ; they are amused thereby, and their interest in phrenology sustained. I do not know that they are any the more able to read character in consequence—if, indeed, they are not somewhat misled by these means. If all brains were of the same quality, texture, health, etc., their use might be more valuable. I do not despise their use. Stratton's "Mathematics of Phrenology" are interesting, his methods of measurement ingenious, and his conclusions go a long way to prove what he wished to prove. Still I am not satisfied. I don't think the soul of man can be pinned in a corner like that, and photographed to a hair's-breadth by any such methods. Where the eye and hand of the intelligent practical phrenologist fail, I am afraid calipers and phreno-physiometers will not be able to succeed. The author of "The Philosophy of Phrenology" says, "The eye and hand are better measurers both of form and size than calipers or any other instrument, and should be made to supersede every such instrument." With this I cordially agree.

5TH QUERY.

Is it possible for a person to have a perfectly healthy brain and yet be idiotic or insane ?

ANSWER.

You can have a perfectly healthy brain in which idiocy is manifested. It may be large or small, but it must be bad in form, low in quality, coarse in structure, or possess some serious organic defect, to be idiotic. In monomania or insanity, disease is always present—disease which not only affects the brain, but may include the whole organization. In the former, imperfect activity of one or two organs; in the latter, intense activity and the actual formation of lesions or tumors on the brain, will be at the basis of the mental derangement whatever it may be. Fifty per cent. of all cases of monomania or hallucination should be curable within an early period, and 25 per cent. of all cases of insanity within twelve months of the date of erratic manifestation. Beyond that period the percentage of recoveries become "small by degrees and beautifully less," as the physical and pathological conditions causing the disease become confirmed. I think the percentage of recoveries is exceedingly small compared to what it should be, owing to the insanity of the authorities,—herding the insane in vast asylums; treating them in groups, instead of phrenologically as individuals, each case on its own merits, and thus hasten their recovery. Thousands suffering from mere delusions and harmless fancies, fine-grained and fine-brained individuals, are incarcerated annually. Many of these are driven into actual insanity by the psychological laws of association and the medical treatment—or, rather, want of it —which such huge concerns must necessarily entail. An idiot may have a perfectly healthy brain, but to one that is insane, health of brain, or of body for that matter, is an impossibility.

6TH QUERY.

If a brain measures 22½ inches first circumference measurement, and 23½ in second circumference measurement —the first being taken with tape around the head at "individuality" and over "parental love," the second over "comparison" and "continuity" —these measurements indicating more the theoretical than the practical talent (page 22), would not the individual, in the direct exercise of the perceptives, evince as much power as one whose head measures 22½ in the first, and 22 inches in the second measurement? That is to say, would his perceptions of "size," "weight," "color," etc., be as correct as one whose brain measured the same in the perceptive brain fibre, but less in the reflective?

ANSWER.

In theory, it is possible to imagine that the individual, in the direct exercise of the perceptive faculties, should evince as much power as another with the same perceptive power but less in the reflectives. But, as a matter of fact, persons so organized do not exercise that direct scrutiny and observation of external things—form, size, color, etc.—as to arrive at as correct conception as the one actually more alert in his perceptives and not over-weighted in his reflectives, as in this case. The principle of size is opposed to the idea that he is at all likely to indulge in the direct exercise of the perceptive faculties. Lord Bacon was a man of large brain, possessing a very high development of the reflective organs, but his judgment was by no means sound where it depended upon his perceiving correctly, collecting correct data from personal observation. It could not be said his perceptives were defective, for the just and proper reason they were not defective ; but his large and powerful reasoning faculties led to their own pre-occupation and natural exercise according to their size, to the exclusion of that direct perception which is referred to in the question.

It is not a fortunate type of brain to have one inch greater in the reflective than in the perceptive, as in this case : it is not favorable to scientific or exact observation. In many instances it must lead to fine-spun theories on sufficient data, and to too much of the metaphysical and transcendental vaporings, veritable " castles in the air," which of late have become so fashionable.

It is natural to look in a well-balanced head for a well-balanced judgment. Such a head referred to would not be of a class favorable to sound judgment in the matter of mere observation. It is one more likely to manifest absentmindedness than alertness in the ordinary affairs of life. Nevertheless, such a person might be highly philosophical, an eminent theologian, moralist, bi-metallist, a peace-society man, a sniffer of the east wind of all ologies, an eminent partisan, but not a man to deal practically with things as they are. He again might see, " in the direct exercise of the perceptive faculties," as correctly as the other to whom you refer, but he could not think the same, and in practice he would act differently, which would amount to the same thing in the end, i. e., the application of his observation : he would see differently.

When a man is found who has just discovered perpetual motion, and who assures you he is about to complete a machine to demonstrate his discovery, see if you cannot find in his coggly top story the only machine you are ever likely to see. It must be remembered such comparisons between two imaginary heads are not profitable, unless indeed it be to excite the faculties of observation when real cases occur, and to perceive the relative size of organs in the same head. In comparing two heads, there are so many things—other things —to be taken into consideration ; quality, health, temperament, youth, age, vitality, activity, excitability— that any judgment predicated on mere size would neither be physiological nor phrenological. To put the whole matter into a nutshell, suppose that " other things being equal," and thus comparing two heads, on safe grounds, I am not disposed to answer your question in the affirmative, as the character of each, based on these measurements, would be totally opposed to their looking at them in a similar manner; their deductions also would be dissimilar.

How is it that practical phrenologists express themselves so differently in the examination of the same head?

ANSWER.

Phrenological examinations will vary according to the individual, and the person giving the examination is differently constituted from another phrenologist examining the same head; and the opinions expressed by each phrenologist will be differently expressed, according to their knowledge of the science, their power of applying it, and ability to express themselves. This is but natural. Phrenologists are not exempted by the science of phrenology, nor by their art of applying it, from the overshadowing law of humanity—viz., difference of organization, brain power, intellectual and moral culture and general capacity. This does not mean that one phrenologist should give a character essentially different from that of another. They must agree on all salient points, although their modes of examination and power of expressing themselves must be somewhat different. If there is an objection in this, the same objection must apply to medicine, law, divinity, or to the physical sciences. If one phrenologist should declare a person had remarkable insight, penetration, force of character, and a well-balanced mind, and another was to declare that the person was a dullard, deficient of insight, lacking penetration, wanting in force of character, a nonenity, either one of them must be lacking not only the qualifications essential to make a good phrenologist, but have a very limp acquaintance with the science of which he professes to be a student. No such difference of opinion would be possible was a scientific knowledge of phrenology the basis of their opinions. Then they would agree, the only difference being in their power to give a just and full meaning to the signs discovered. In my opinion the differences of opinion amongst phrenologists are more apparent than real, arising from their individual application of the science, not from their inability to apply it. One has a lucid manner, another full and verbose, another terse and contracted, and so on; but all agree on salient points, while their modes of expression vary.

Now that the British Phrenological Association is fully established, its lecturers, examiners, and teachers will, in all probability, adopt a more uniform method of procedure, which might present some advantages. But no amount of uniformity can obscure individuality, latent tact, or special power. Churches have attempted this and failed; trade unions have tried it to their disaster; while it has ever been, and will be, the weak point in communism and all social movements based on an imperfect knowledge of what equality and uniformity truly means. The most perfect unity and harmony, is ever found in variety.

This is Nature's law, and must be right. As phrenologists differ in character, ability, and powers of expression, so will their manner and style of discerning character, making deductions therefrom, giving suitable advice, be different.

8TH QUERY.

It appears to me that in examining heads the greatest difficulty is not so much measurements as to ascertain the entire leading or sum of the character, from combining the various faculties. It seems to me a man with large benevolence and equally large acquisitiveness, would not be so generous as one having large benevolence only. Is that so?

ANSWER.

It is true that men like Eustace or Gosse may give freely and fully, having large sympathies and powerful feelings of reverence, spirituality, and generosity, and comparatively little of what is called acquisitiveness. But, lacking the latter, they would be more benevolent, I deny. They might give more foolishly, freely, and sympathetically, I admit; thereby gratifying the feeling or impulse of benevolence. Acquisitiveness is as essential to personal generosity as it is to common-sense. It is absolutely requisite to true giving; it knows the value of getting.

As a student of phrenology, it is requisite that you should understand the location and function of each individual organ so far as these have been discovered. Next view them in combination, and their effect in combination or character. I take this to be your meaning. Elsewhere I have divided the head into three regions, and these regions into sub-divisions. Now, if any of these regions predominate, it is an easy matter to estimate its influence on character. It will predominate. Benevolence is a sentiment; acquisitiveness is less a sentiment than a propensity. When both are large, acquisitiveness will rob benevolence of its softness, not sense. Benevolence will take the crashness and meanness out of the mere desire to acquire, and give at least one useful outlet for its acquisitions. John Bright was large in benevolence, also large in acquisitiveness. He did not scatter like a prodigal, nor gather like a miser or a fool. The intellectual character, for instance, will be affected as the observing, knowing, or reflective faculties are in the ascendant; whether the moral region is strong or weak, the social or domestic region less or more powerful. No mere supposing of cases will be helpful; nothing but practice and experience will do in the consulting-room. It is for this reason, more than any other, a phrenologist should be endowed with special gifts for his calling; and not the least of these is sagacity, natural intellectual ability, intuition, and keen powers of observation, thoughtfulness, and judgment. Some hints can be obtained from a teacher of experience, and some useful suggestions may be found in most of our text books.

9TH QUERY.

It has been stated that children's heads are larger in the perceptive than in the reflective **organs**. My observations do not **confirm** this. If we say the perceptives **are** the most active, are we right? **Is the** apparent deficiency due **to** the frontal sinus being undeveloped? Does the foregoing affect the usual measurements? **Is** there **any** special method adopted **in the** measurement and examination **of the** heads of children? **Should we give** advice in very **young children as** to the "**choice of pursuits?**"

ANSWER.

In the majority of cases the perceptive faculties are larger in children than the reflective. They are always more active than the reflective. Children learn to see and to distinguish one object from another, one person from another, before they can be said to think or reason. Not that they do not think in their little way. Universally you will find that the language of childhood corresponds with the development and activity of the perceptives : " Let me see," " Where is it ?" " Oh, see ! " " Come and see," " What's this ? " and " What for ? " are common modes of expression. Some children being more observant and sharper than others, their language, actions and mannerisms will correspond therewith. The absence of the frontal sinus in children certainly does make some slight difference in the formation of the head, and constitutes

somewhat **to the** apparent deficiency **spoken of. The** absence of the sinus enables us **the more** accurately to observe the form **of the** brain. The character of **the children** will correspond to that **form, and the** varying shades of that form **in the** course of brain development and **cranial** growth.

The perceptive organs are **all** small, but **are** kept in constant activity (where **there** is sight) from the cradle to the grave. They are more fully supplied with nerve cells, nerve fibres, and infinitely smaller **arteries, than** the larger organs which **are** brought into play afterward. These (the perceptive organs) are most **active in** children, some **of whose days are passed in** seeing and wanting to see wonder after wonder in this world of wonders to **them.**

The mental operations of childhood are **those of observation—memory** of the observed and **heard,** and comparison **of the same** ; imitation, or endeavor **to** reproduce the same ; imagination, or the mental reproduction **of** what it has seen, heard, or **imperfectly** realized, etc., variously **modified.** The mental progress **of** unfoldment conforms to the phrenological development. It is only in a less degree the child **is the** man. It observes, reasons, and reflects according to brain capacity, size, or development, brain quality, fineness, density, **weight,** and activity. The child sees, hears, **and** thinks. It detects sounds, and **distinguishes** lights and shadows ; **detects** familiar objects and expressions at a very early period. Its faculties of observation **are** engrossed by object lessons in everything by which it is surrounded. It keenly notices, greedily listens, remembers, and repeats. All this world is for it a veritable wonderland—a place of fairies. It dreads the strange, and is drawn by the known and loved; and all these things primarily excite into activity the perceptive faculties, and in a minor degree the reasoning and imaginative faculties. It wants to see more. Not only is this so, but where children show the least aptitude for noticing, they are drawn out upon all occasions by parents, guardians, and friends. So, with the exception of "alimentiveness" (and the automatic action of certain organs—nerve centres—not adequately known, but localized in the base of the brain), the perceptive organs are the most active in childhood, the first matured in manhood, and almost the first to show decline in old age. Next to the perceptive organs in childhood, "comparison" and "eventuality" are correspondingly active. Higher up "imitation" and "wonder" come into play. Then "ideality" with "comparison;" "imitation" with "comparison." Below "comparison," "eventuality" bulges out the forehead, and gives that rotund form to the forehead above the perceptives which gives the impression that the reflectives are relatively larger than the perceptives. It does appear to me that in babyhood and in childhood, eventuality occupies the major portion of the forehead, and that the organs of comparison and causality—especially the latter—do not fully come into play until the forehead rises and expands

more fully in the superior region. The love and trust of childhood are colored largely by its posterior brain, in which parental love occupies a similar position to that of eventuality in the anterior brain. Childhood reflects, but not in that sense or in any form which shows that the reflectives are larger than the perceptives. You will notice the growth of childhood's powers is something like this. Automatic and instinctive; "alimentiveness;" the noticing and detecting familiar sounds; observing more fully; attempting to reproduce familiar sounds; endearments, exhibiting a desire to possess; memory and "comparison;" attachment, "comparison" and "imitation," desire for notice and endearment, talent, "causality," and "approbativeness" budding forth—especially the latter—the back head being larger than the front head.

As to measurements, I do not think you will find upon more careful observation anything to alter the proportionate measurements. In some instances you may find eventuality and comparison larger than the perceptives. In such cases, you will find imaginative and inaccurate representations of things observed according as these organs may be influenced.

I apply the same measurements to childhood as I do to the healthy adult, bearing in mind that the texture of the brain in childhood is not so confirmed as in later life; also what is most likely to be exercised according to the foregoing.

As to advice about "choice of pursuits," it is best to be guided by individual cases. As a rule, advice for physical culture, health, and upbringing till seven ; best of school training and discipline up till 12 to 14 years, with hints as to pursuits ; the educational training to be in the direction of the pursuits, and from 12, or thereabout, on the " choice of pursuits " in a more definite form. As the child is father of the man, some will have a decided predilection for some things, others no special leaning. According to your ability advise and aid the parents to a wise selection.

As an aid in giving advice upon " choice of pursuits," you would do well to know something of the parents' circumstances, means for education and preferment at their disposal ; the nature of local enterprises and opportunities in district for affording employment. You may know what a person can do : by the above aid you may know where he **can do it.** This has been, in a measure, replied to under the 1st question.

10TH QUERY.

What are the best busts and books for students of phrenology ? What is the best way to get into practice ?

ANSWER.

I have indicated in " **Practical Phrenology** " the busts and books. For beginners I would recommend Fowler's china bust, " Key " or " Register," and his " Self-instructor,"

" Manual of Phrenology." For more advanced pupils, Nicholas Morgan's bust, and the plaster model of the human skull, both recently published by Vago, their respective keys, the foregoing works, and Dr. Donovan's " Handbook of Phrenology," " Combe's Works," and an Art and Science Course in Physiology and Anatomy ; reading and study should be accompanied by practice.

For professional examiners, the largest possible acquaintance with the literature of their profession, and " current events," will form a good liberal education, and inspired by an humble devotion to understand and ennoble human nature, and attachment to their work, will be certain to provide plenty of opportunities of testing the science in public and private.

The best way to get into practice, is to practice freely as an amateur, giving delineations where and when possible. In this way a certain amount of proficiency in observation, manipulation, deduction, and expression is insured. Another method is, to become for a time an assistant to some well-known examiner.

In conclusion, it is essential, however well-educated the phrenological aspirant may be, nothing short of a good, practical course " by the living voice "—demonstration—will be of real service to him ; with this a professional career is only a matter of

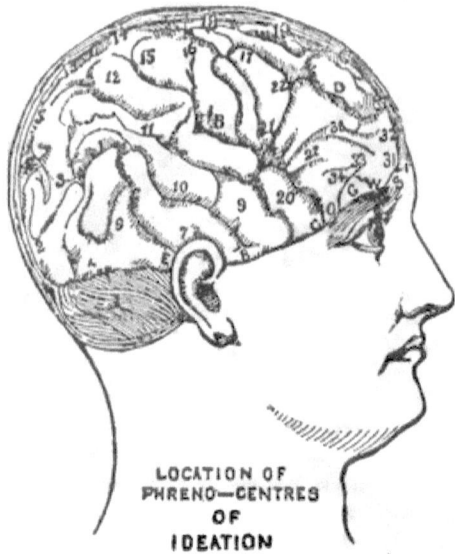

**LOCATION OF
PHRENO—CENTRES
OF
IDEATION**

GENERAL PRINCIPLES.

The Brain is the chief organ of the mind. The body as a whole manifests mind. As is brain and body, or organization, so is mind.

The Brain " is not a simple unit, but a collection of many peculiar instruments," called organs or centres. Neither is the mind a unit, but the sum of many faculties.

The Brain is subject to growth, the mind is subject to development. Arrested growth in the one means imperfect development of the other, contrariwise, otherwise, etc.

The Skull in life as perfectly conforms anatomically to the formation of

NOTE.—The Organs—centres—are all double, each faculty of the mind having two lying at corresponding locations in the cerebral hemispheres. The above ideal map presenting those of the right hemisphere of the cerebrum and cerebellum only.

the brain as bark to a tree or skin to the hand. The size, form, and power of the brain can be thoroughly gauged by the examination of the skull.

The Body in life, in color, size, form and texture, adequately presents the health, quality, and physiological traits likely to modify the manifestations of mind as indicated by the skull.

There are no manifestations of mind without their physical correlatives. Some minds are dominated by the body ; are creatures of passion, impulse, appetite, and sense. In others the mind is supreme, the bodily influences being subordinate; that is, under the direction of the mind.

To read character, it is necessary to take into consideration the Brain, the organs or centres, their size, function, and combination, the quality of organization as a whole, and the influence of health, temperament, and education.

Exclude the foregoing from any system of mental science, and it is impossible for the mind to be investigated or human character made possible of analysis.

LOCATION AND DEFINITION OF PHRENO-CENTRES.

1.—*Domestic Feelings or Propensities.*

These are common to man and animals, the Phreno-centres of which are located in the cerebellum and posterior lobes of the cerebrum. Their width and fulness give corresponding conformation to the cranium in the occiput.

See *Numbers :—*

1.—Amative Centre—(Motor Centre of Co-ordination)—Instinct of sexual love, affection.

A —Pairing   "   **Conjugal** love, oneness of affection

2.—Parental   "   Desire for and love of offspring **and** all **young.**

3.—Gregarious   "   **Friendship, sociability,** gregariousness.

4.—**Inhabitive**   "   **Love of** home and country.

5.—Concentrative "   Continuity, application, consecu-**tiveness.**

SELF-PROTECTIVE **FEELINGS OR SENTI-MENTS.**

These are common to man and some animals, and are located in the parietal and temporal **lobes** of the cerebrum. Their form **and size** give width to the cranium at **the parietal** walls ; superior, anterior, **and posterior** to the *meatus auditus.*

E —Vitative Centre—Disease and Death-resisting instinct—love of life.

6.—Combative   "   Prompts to resistance, defence, courage.

7.—Executive   "   (Motor centre of Energy)—Resistance, **Executive-ness.**

8.—Alimentive "   (Motor **centre** of Taste)—Appetite for food, etc.

9.—Acquisitive   "   (Motor centre **of Pre-**hension)—**Desire** to get, economy.

10.—Secretive   "   (**Motor** centre of Hearing) — Concealment of thought, self restraint, policy.

11.—Watchful   "   **Cautiousness,** guard-**edness,** apprehensiveness of consequences.

II.—Self-Regarding Sentiments or Egotistic Feelings.

These centres are located in the superior and coronal convolutions of the cerebrum, and give height and fulness to the cranium.

12.—Approbative Centre.—Regard for the opinion of others, de-**sire for ap-proval, love of** praise.

13.—Self-respective   "   A proper appreciation of self, self-respect, **dignity.**

14.—Self-assertive   "   (Motor centre of Locomotion) —Perseverance, will, decision of character.

III.—Moral and Spiritual Sentiments, or Feelings proper to Man.

These centres are located in the superior coronal regions of the brain. Their full development gives corresponding conformation to the cranium.

15.—Justice Centre.—Sentiment of right, conscientiousness, respect for the rights of others.

16.—Hope " Anticipation of good, faith, expectation.

17.—Spirituality " Belief in the unseen, love of the marvelous, the occult.

18.—Veneration " Respect for authority, regard for greatness seen and unseen, worshipping instinct.

(Veneration, Hope, and Spirituality combined give origin to religion. Their perversion promotes the follies of superstition and the vagaries of modern occultism and spiritism, etc.)

19.—Sympathetic Centre.—Sentiments of generous instincts, sympathy, kindness.

IV.—*Semi-Intellectual Feelings or Sentiments.*

These are proper to man, and are expressive of mental forces which are not purely intellectual on the one hand, neither are they mere feelings or instincts on the other. They are located in the superior temporal and parietal lobes of the brain. Their full development gives extension to the cranium in the superior anterior regions.

20.—Constructive Centre.—(This should be classified as an instinct) —Desire to make, construct, put together.

21.—Ideal " (Ferrier's centre of head and eyes)—Love of the beautiful, poetic, sense and enjoyment of perfection.

22b.—Sublime " (Ferrier's centre of forearm) —Love of the terrific, majestic, grand, and vast in nature.

22.—Imitative " Faculty of mental reproduction, mimicry, aptitude, alertness to copy.

23.—Mirth Loving " Sense of humorous and the ludicrous, fun, wit, facetiousness.

INTELLECTUAL FACULTIES.

V.—The *Senses*—Feeling or touch, taste, smell, hearing, and sight, place man in sensuous communication with the external world and his fellows.

THE PERCEPTIVE CENTRES.

VI.—The *Perceptive Centres* (possessed by animals relatively inferior in power and manifestation to man) are located in man in the inferior anterior cerebral lobes. The full development gives width and fulness to the lower forehead.

I.—Individualizing Centre.—The desire to perceive, see, pick out, to observe.

figuration, memory of **faces**, l o o k s, persons, etc.

S.—Size " Perception of divergencies in quantity, adjectives, large, small, moderate, etc.

W.—Weight Centre.—(Connected with the cerebellum) — Perception of distances, desire to balance, control of motion.

C.—Color " Sense of color, discernment and love of color.

O —Order " Perception of method, education, order and system.

VII.—LITERARY CENTRES, OR KNOWING FACULTIES.

These centres are for the manifestation of those faculties of the human mind which perceive the relations of external objects. They are located midway between the centres of the perceptive and the reasoning faculties. Their full development gives width and fulness to the centre forehead.

C.—Calculation Centre.—Perception of numbers, talent for reckoning.

L.—Localizing " The geographical and traveling instinct, recollection of

traditional instinct, "What our **fathers** did," memory of events **and facts.**

33.—Time " Sense of the lapse of moments, intervals, **when, dates.**

34.—Tune " Sense of harmonious sounds, music.

L.—Language " "The gift of tongues," the faculty of reducing thoughts to words, speech.

VIII.—THE REASONING CENTRES.

These are the faculties of the human mind which compare, judge and discriminate. It may be said they are not common to animals, but are common to man. The centres of these faculties are located in the superior anterior brain. Their full development gives fulness and width to the upper forehead.

36.—**Causality** Centre.—"Traces the dependences of phenomena, and the relation of cause and effect," thinking and originality.

37.—Comparison " The mental faculty of discernment and inference. It discerns analogies, resemblances, and differences.

C.—Intuitive " Spiritual and sagacious discernment of mental and moral powers.

D.—Suavity " Geniality, blandness,

No attempt has been made to accurately class the various centres. The above is, as all classification must be, an approximation. Phreno-centres, related to each other in function, are grouped together in the brain ; but, even in this grouping, they insensibly impinge on one another—influence one another.

In like manner do the faculties of the mind combine. Thus for Memory, Will, and Judgment, there are no external signs. These are qualities of the mind which depend for their manifestation on certain combinations of the faculties. The tyro in phrenology may call Eventuality the organ of memory, Firmness the organ of will, Causality the organ of judgment. These are gross errors, into which no educated phrenologist would fall, and in expression carefully avoid.

THE END.